Steamy Romance Opens Hotwife's Eyes - A Hot Wife Sordid Affair Wife Sharing Romance Novel

Karly Violet

Published by Karly Violet, 2020.

This is a work of fiction. Similarities to real people, places, or events are entirely coincidental.

STEAMY ROMANCE OPENS HOTWIFE'S EYES - A HOT WIFE SORDID AFFAIR WIFE SHARING ROMANCE NOVEL

First edition. October 20, 2020.

ISBN: 979-8201905309

Written by Karly Violet.

Sign up to my Patreon account and receive exclusive
Hotwife stories every month and sexy scenes every week!
https://www.patreon.com/karlyviolet

Chapter One: Pics for Pics

For ten years, I have been married to a beautiful woman. As a matter of fact, most would concede that Lauren is the perfect woman for a guy like me. She's sweet, passionate, and athletic to a fault. Hitting the gym three or four times each week, my wife of ten years has kept her abs toned and her body fit enough that when we have sex she can do things that most other women would cringe at the thought of doing. So, as a guy lucky enough to be able to fuck a woman like Lauren, you would think that I would be satisfied. Unfortunately, that's just not the case. I want more.

"I'll trade one for one," I tell the guy on the other end of our text conversation. Last week I put out an advertisement on an adult website seeking pictures of other women, preferably wives. In trade, I stated that I am willing to give an equal number of pictures that I've taken of Lauren. Of course, all pics are nudes and I feel just a little guilty about doing this behind her back, but she would never agree. My wife likes sex just fine, but she likes it with only me. There has been no interest on her part to either show other men what she has or to take part in any sex act with another guy. I've begged her to at least consider giving another man a blow job or a hand job, but Lauren has been steadfastly opposed the entire time. So, I've decided to settle for this little bit of naughtiness instead.

"I'm good with that." A moment later, my cell phone receives an image file from the man I'm texting with. I open it and see a lovely woman in her early thirties completely naked with her medium-sized breasts firm and sitting very nicely upon her chest. A small line of pubic hair moves from the top of her slit for about two inches in a way that lets me know that the curtains don't necessarily match the drapes. His wife has her legs parted just enough that I can see her puffy, pink labia and clitoral hood as I expand the image on my phone's screen.

"You have a nice-looking wife," I reply.

"Thanks. Your turn." I grin to myself as I select a similar picture of Lauren to send to him. It takes only a moment or so for the image file to transfer to him and only a few moments more before he comments on my wife.

"She's fucking hot." An emoji smile pops up next and then another less family friendly emoji that appears to be a man's hard cock. "I'm going to beat off to her," he tells me in his next message.

"Have fun." I don't receive any further messages from him, but I open the image of my wife to have a good look at it myself. "Fuck, Lauren," I moan as I reach into my shorts and touch my stiff rod. "You're a hot little minx." My wife is absolutely an attractive woman, just thirty years old and sporting a pair of C-cup breasts that have never been touched by a surgeon's scalpel. There are women in the world who would kill someone to have the natural shape that Lauren has in her breasts, and a far greater number of men who would do anything to touch them. Even so, the idea of letting guys see my wife naked isn't entirely the only thing driving me to share her pictures. It's the fact that she has no clue that I'm letting other men see her that turns me on the most. My wife is a modest prude, and she barely allowed me to take the half-dozen or so nude pictures of her that I have now. As a matter of fact, I have led her to believe that they have all since been deleted.

"Hey, have you got any more pics?" Another text message comes across my cell phone. It's a different guy than the one I was only just dealing with a moment ago.

"Maybe," I reply. "Which guy are you?"

"Tim212," he says almost immediately. I remember this one. He asked for pics yesterday and I've sent him all but one of my wife's nude pics already.

"I have one more, a close-up pussy shot. What have you got for trade?"

I wait a minute or so for a reply before he responds, "My wife, full nude, with face." I begin to get hard. Sure, it's fun to see other women's breasts and pussies, but the idea of getting a full-frontal pic *with* her face is the holy grail of wife pic swaps. This is especially true since all the guys who have contacted me about pictures are supposedly in the same town as I am. With a population of a couple of hundred thousand, there is a slight possibility that if you see a woman's face on a nude pic it could be someone you know.

"Okay," I reply as I begin the wait. Within another minute, I have the image on my phone and I open it to look at it. "Holy cow," I reply to the man who sent it. Sure enough, the young woman's face is fully visible, her blue eyes and blonde hair every bit as attractive as anything else on her body. This picture includes the same small, perky breasts along with a waxed or shaven beaver and a tattoo just above the bikini line. I pull at my engorged pecker as I look the woman over.

"Send, please?" I'm interrupted by the text message as I ogle the man's wife.

"Here it comes." I upload Lauren's pussy pic, remarkably clear for most pictures of women's private parts. Everything about my wife's lovely snatch is easy to see, including its light pink color along her beefy labia and her long, dangly clitoris and hood. She has a hairless mouthful of muff at 4k resolution that any man could enjoy. Lauren is a woman worth the effort to fuck.

"Damn, man," is the man's reply. "She's got a nice one, doesn't she?"

"She sure does," I answer him. "It tastes and feels as nice as it looks."

"Fucking awesome." Several emoji's pop up as he finishes his text. It's the same sort of thing I've seen before, over and over again, as I've shared Lauren's pictures with dozens of men this way. "I would love to taste that."

"Yeah, I wish you could," I joke with him.

"Can I?" I chuckle at first as I read his text message back to me. Of course he can't; my wife wouldn't do something like that.

"I wish you could," I say again. "But wifey isn't receptive to that sort of thing."

I shake my head and start to put the phone back into my pocket just as another text message from him comes through. "Don't tell her."

What? Don't tell my wife about fucking another man, just have her *do it?* I shake my head. "She would have to know. That's the way it works when a guy and girl fuck, man."

"Blindfold her."

"What?" I follow this text with my own emoji's, one of them representing someone completely out of their mind.

"Just take her to a hotel in town and tell her you want to do something kinky. Blindfold her. Then I come in. She doesn't have to know." I get hard as I read his text to me. Could that really work? Could I just take Lauren to a hotel and have her stripped naked and on the bed blindfolded?

"She knows how my skin feels. She'll know it's a stranger as soon as her hands touch your back."

"Gloves, man. Sensuous, satiny gloves. Have her wear those and handcuff her to the bed. Tell her it's a weird fetish you want her to roleplay with you. She'll love it." Three smiling emoji's follow this text as I begin to shake. The thought of it nearly puts me over as I pull on my pre-coming penis.

"I don't know. I'll think about it, okay? Until then, can you send a pic of you?"

"Sure, but no face, okay?" he replies quickly. "I'll give you a headless nude of me." In just seconds I receive the file and open it on my phone. The man is fit, with a toned abdomen and absolutely no body hair, including around his stiff manhood.

"There's a problem here. I have pubes and you don't. She'll notice."

"Shave, dude," is his reply. "Do it before you take her to the hotel, maybe even today, and tell her that you're trying something new. You'll like it."

I consider what the stranger is suggesting as I begin to stroke my penis. Could this work? Would Lauren really not know that another man was eating her out or even fucking her? I've seen similar videos online of women being fucked like this, but most I would think are staged for the camera. I'm not sure how she would react to being seen or screwed by a stranger if Lauren were to somehow find out. "I'll think about it and let you know later, okay?"

"Sure." That's the end of our text message conversation as I close the text window on my cell phone. Getting up from the small stool in our bathroom, I tuck my phone into a pocket on the side of my shorts and flush the toilet. I'm sure Lauren has been waiting to get in here for the past few minutes as I've taken a little time to myself in our master bathroom.

"Well, good morning," my wife says to me with a smile on her face from our bed. "You've been in there for a while. Are you feeling okay?"

I rub a hand over my stomach and reply, "Dinner was a little rough on me."

"Oh, I'm sorry." I lie down in bed with Lauren and look into her green eyes as she continues to look with concern upon me.

"Plus, I had to send your nude pics to a few guys so that they could look them over." The momentary look of horror on my wife's face is priceless.

Lauren laughs a little and says, "You deleted those, Robert." I begin to laugh with her as my cock gets hard again. I like to tease her with fragments of truth, or peeks at what I'm actually up to behind her back. There have been a couple of times that I've gone to see escorts when I've been on business trips during our marriage to let off a little sexual tension and I've even told Lauren in the midst of our times during sex that I've paid women for sex. She never believes me, always thinking that I'm just doing a little roleplay for the sake of our intimate time together. My wife is none the wiser about my sexual yearnings, including my incessant porn watching and occasional tryst with a paid whore, and that makes confessing to her so much more erotic. If, however, Lauren were to ever discover that I'm telling her the truth, I'm afraid our marriage would be over. She's threatened as much in the past while joking around with me.

"Yeah, I deleted them," I lie for the umpteenth time. "But it would be funny if I ever did share something like that with another guy or two."

"Don't you ever," she replies with a final snort. "I couldn't bear the thought of a stranger looking at my naked body." Maybe she couldn't, but I certainly could. If it weren't for that little bit of fucking around behind her back, I'm afraid that I might go full-bore into looking for a woman to fuck steadily. It's not that our marriage is an unhappy one, mind you, but it's a little too dry for my liking. Lauren is not the sort to get worked up into a sexual frenzy unless she's three seconds from an orgasm. I'm convinced that if I could bring another man into our bedroom at that very moment, Lauren would agree to let him fuck her. The only problem is, I don't know any guys who could enter the room, mount her, and come within three seconds.

"I've got to get up," I say as I stand up from the bed.

"You're hard," my wife quips at me as she looks up. "Don't you want me to take care of that for you?"

"Maybe sixty-nine?" I say with a smile.

Lauren frowns. "You know I don't like that, Robert. You gag me too much and you get a little too excited."

"It's sex, honey. We're supposed to both be excited to be involved in it." I shake my head as I go to the closet to pick out some clothes for the day. It's Saturday, so I figure I'll probably end up on a golf course with my buddies.

"Yeah, but you get a little *too* excited." It's always the same with my wife. She likes sex straightforward, missionary position, and quick. Fucking is a five-minute adventure for the two of us, our orgasms just a means by which to try to erase a day of stress for the two of us, nothing more. There is no connection anymore when I come inside Lauren, which is why I've started penetrating her anally. She doesn't like it, and at first she screamed at me for doing it at all, but now she tolerates it once in a great while. I guess my wife figures that if it takes my mind off asking her to fuck another guy it's worth it.

"Sorry," I mumble as I get my things together.

"It's okay," she says as she smiles at me. "I'll get you trained yet." I grimace as I continue getting ready. How do I answer something like that? For a *decade* she's told me that she would eventually get me *trained* to be the husband she's always wanted, and I guess we're close to that point now. Sex is scheduled and well-defined. Anything outside of what has become standard operating procedure during our coital interludes is not to be discussed. At least, not seriously.

"I'll see you this afternoon. I'm heading out to golf."

"Be back by dinner, okay? Barb and Hutton are coming over." I nod and walk out of the room with my golf clothing after sliding into a pair of shorts and a tee shirt. There's no need to put on the other stuff until after I have checked into the club and gotten to my locker. If I can't have any sex this morning, at least I can enjoy breakfast with the guys. It's a poor substitute, I know, but it is a substitute. For now.

Chapter Two: Persistence is a Virtue

12

"Have you thought it over?" I look at the text message as I finish grilling the pork ribs on the barbecue outside the house. It's been more than a day since I told the stranger I would consider his plan to meet and play with my wife, and I've given it some thought. It's just that I can't see a way around the plethora of excuses Lauren will give me when I tell her I simply want to go stay at a hotel for a night. With no kids or family nearby to pester us at our home, she would wonder why I would even want to pay to go somewhere else to act out a fetish. She knows me all too well; I'm not big on spending money for nothing.

"I have and I don't think I can get her to go along with going to a hotel." I shake my head as I send the message. The fact is, I would have loved to have done something like this, but Lauren just wouldn't go along with it.

"Do you have a mailing address? It can be a mailbox away from home or even an email address. I have something to send you that might change her mind."

"Okay," I answer back as I think about this. "I'm not sure I want to give you my place of residence."

"Email?" Of course, I have an email address that I use to sign into porn sites, so I give him that address in the next text message I send. "What is this about?"

"Hang on." I continue to cook the pork ribs on my grill as I tuck my phone into my pocket. About five minutes later, I get another text from the man that asks me to check my email. I log into that account from my phone and the top mail I have is from the Dunsten Hotel in town. I open it up.

"One room, king bed, paid for."

"Really?" I look at the receipt and notice that it has, in fact, been paid for by someone else. "This is for tonight?" There's no way I can put something together so quickly. Surely this guy knows that a guy like me can't just tell his wife that we have to immediately get ready and come to the hotel. Besides, we both have work tomorrow.

"Tonight," he answers back. "Read to the bottom." I continue to look at the email and notice that also included is a second trip to another resort outside of town for two nights if we go and try out the room. The hotel has recently had several upgrades made during its renovation, and I've heard that they are giving away rooms and offering more to get people to try it out. However, I've also heard that the rooms have been sold out for months in advance.

"I don't know." Shaking my head, I look over at Lauren. She's sitting on the patio in the shade waiting for me to finish the pork ribs. I've promised her this meal for the past couple of weeks, and she really enjoys my cooking, which is another reason I don't think this will work. It's two in the afternoon, so getting our meal over with and getting ready will take some doing.

"You'll love it, I promise." The guy is persistent as hell as he keeps trying to get me to commit. Closing the top of the grill, I walk over to my wife and look down at her.

"Lauren, I have a surprise."

My wife looks up at me through her sunglasses. "A surprise?" She smiles, obviously expecting something that will completely thrill her, like an expensive piece of jewelry or a bouquet of flowers. "We're both taking off from work tomorrow."

"What?" She giggles a little as she shakes her head. "Neither one of us can just call in or not show up, Robert. You know how it goes for the both of us." My wife is an attorney for a company in town and I'm a bank vice president at a branch not too far from where she works. We both make good money at jobs that are not all that difficult. As a matter of fact, neither one of us hardly ever misses, and rarely would something like that even happen at the same time. We can both be workaholics, and so cutting out of work the day before or the day of work is not something we're accustomed to doing.

"No, really. I entered a contest a couple of months ago, and totally forgot about it until just now." I hold up my phone so that she can see the opened email. "The Dunsten is open again, and we have been given a free night to stay in one of their nicer rooms." I shake as I study the expression on Lauren's face.

"You can't be serious. Are they only just now telling you that this is for tonight?" My wife has noticed the reservation starting at five this afternoon.

"It was in my spam email folder," I reply as I pull the phone back. "I guess it got in there by mistake."

"This could just be a hoax, sweetheart. If it's in the spam folder, it's probably not legitimate." My wife's legal mind in action, already debunking my attempts to get her to the room for a little fun.

"It's not. I called a little while ago and they confirmed it. It's for tonight and they can't move it."

Lauren pulls her sunglasses off to look at me directly. "Robert, if we did this we would miss work tomorrow and I would end up with that much more on my plate to take care of on Tuesday. I don't think this is such a good idea."

"Then I'll go without you," I say in a huff as I walk away.

"What do you mean, *without* me? That's a little insensitive, don't you think?"

"How is it insensitive? You don't want to go anyway. All you want to do is sit around here and have a bit of barbecue before heading into work tomorrow. It's all we do anymore, Lauren. Work, work, work, and then have a bland weekend. Repeat the next week. When will we do something a little spontaneous?"

"Spontaneous?" My wife looks me over. "I know you like to fancy yourself as the spontaneous type, my dear, but you are not exactly the poster child for spontaneous." She chuckles a little as I walk past her and go into the house. "Where are you going?"

"Fifteen minutes," I say as I close the door. I hope she understands that is how long she has before the ribs need to come off the grill. Either way, I don't care whether they burn or not. I'm tired of being told by her that I don't act spontaneously. It's not the first time she's pegged me this way about something like this and it probably won't be the last, but I'm going to prove her wrong right now.

"Where are you going?" she calls out to me as I walk into our bathroom and shut the door.

"You'll see," I answer as I turn on the shower and begin to take off my clothes.

"You're scaring me," my wife says as she stands at the bathroom door. "Unlock this door and let me in, okay?" I ignore her as I step into the shower and lather up. Then, borrowing her razor from the little holder on the wall, I begin to shave my pubic hairs off. "Robert, say something, please."

"I'm fine," I call out as I work to get everything zipped off from around my hard penis and ball sack. Something about deciding to commit to what the stranger told me to do makes me horny as I remove all the pubic hairs from my crotch. "Wait until you see this."

"Robert, you need to come out here."

"Check the ribs," I say back as I finish up. "They'll burn."

"Fuck the ribs." We have a bathroom key in my top dresser drawer, where we keep a lot of things we want to hide, and I am almost certain I can hear Lauren open and close the drawer. Then the doorknob begins to rattle a bit.

"Are you breaking in here?" I ask as I turn off the shower and grab a towel.

"Robert, you shouldn't scare me like this." The door suddenly opens and in pops my wife. "Why the hell did you lock this door?"

"I wanted to take a shower," I answer defiantly. "Also, I like privacy when I'm in a bathroom."

"Privacy? We're *married,* Robert. Whatever you have I've already seen."

"Oh, really?" I drop the towel to the floor as a wicked grin crosses my face. "Have you seen this before?"

"*Shit,* honey!" Lauren's eyes lock onto my groin, which is now hairless. "What have you done?"

"I thought I would try something different, especially since you claim I can't be spontaneous."

"But, Rob..." My wife gasps as she continues to look at me. "That's not the way I've ever pictured you to look."

"Yeah, I would say this is pretty fucking spontaneous, wouldn't you?" I walk past her as my hard staff waggles from side to side. I really want to try out my newly-shorn piece of equipment on Lauren, but I also want to allow our sexual tension to build as I try to convince her that we need to go stay the night in the renovated hotel. "So, I'm going tonight, and someone's going to experience this. Will it be you?" I grin again as I grip my penis with my hand.

"Shit," she says as she smiles back at me. "Are you really serious about this? Do you really want to go stay the night in a hotel that's only ten miles away?"

"Just for fun," I reply as I walk up to Lauren. "We've not had a romantic getaway for a long time. Plus, we could get a little kinky while we do it."

"Kinky?" My wife shakes her head. "I don't know how kinky I'm willing to be, but just getting away for an evening could be fun."

"It'll be great," I promise as I run a hand along her face. "Let's give it a try, okay? Just for tonight."

"Just tonight?"

"Well, plus the additional two nights we get for going to the hotel tonight. It's in the email. We get two nights at a resort out of state if we do this tonight."

"There's got to be a catch," Lauren says as she backs away from me. "What's the catch?"

"We have to sit through a little presentation this evening and sign up for the other trip. That's all there is to it."

"I don't know."

"Lauren, fuck, just let go and do it, okay?" I shake my head as I pull on a pair of shorts and a tee shirt. The ribs, by now, are probably a little on the well-done side of cooking and I need to get them off as soon as I can.

"Fine," she says with a smile. "We'll eat and then go. Happy?"

I smile and turn to give her a kiss on the cheek. "Very." We go outside to enjoy the next hour as we eat pork ribs and baked potatoes, not long after leaving messages with our employers that we will be out due to unexpected circumstances. Neither one of us will be suspected of anything out of order with our work, and things will resume as normal on Tuesday. It's one night in which I am going to let another man enjoy the taste of my wife. A night that will help to fulfill at least one fantasy I've had for years concerning Lauren.

Chapter Three: Trust and Secrecy

"This is a really nice hotel," Lauren says as we walk into the room. "And we really don't have to pay for this at all?"

"Not a penny," I assure her. "And apparently they even waved the little meeting they wanted us to go to later tonight." It had been a lie on my part anyway, one that would help to justify why we were being given a free room in a four-star hotel. "They just want us to fill out the survey tomorrow morning before we leave."

"Well, my survey will definitely comment on how lovely this place is." Lauren goes to the king-size bed and has a seat on the end of it. "So, what are we going to be doing in here, my love?" This is more playful than I've seen my wife in some time. It's nice to see her behave in a way that's more along the lines of the woman I married a decade ago.

"Here," I say as I hand her a small black bag. "You'll wear this later, okay?"

Lauren pulls out a black sleeping mask and a small black nightie. "Oh, Robert, this is a little naughty, isn't it?"

"A little," I concur with a smile. "It will be fun, though. Just go take a shower and then put that on. I'll be ready for you in here."

"Okay." Lauren smiles as she turns and goes to the bathroom. I pull my cell phone from my pocket.

"We're here," I text the stranger on the other end. "She is in the bathroom to shower and get ready."

"Good," he texts back to me. "I'm in the lobby." My heart pounds as I think about it. Suddenly, this is becoming much more real than it has been up until this point. "Tell me when you're ready. And remember, give her the earbuds and have her listen to music. That will make it less likely that she'll know what's going on."

"Yeah," I reply. "I'll have her ready. Just be careful and do things like I told you. She knows me really well."

"No problem." It's the end of our texting and I begin to work on getting the bed ready for my wife.

"How do I look?" she asks me as she walks into the room half an hour later.

"Oh, wow," I reply as I look at the tight little black thing she's wearing. There's little left to the imagination as I see her light-colored nipples through the thin black lace of the outfit. "I thought it would look good on you, but I had no idea it would look *this* good."

"Thank you," Lauren says with a smile as she looks over at the bed. "Handcuffs, Robert? Really?"

"Just for kicks." I wave a hand toward the bed and she goes to lie down. "Just lie back and I'll get you ready."

"Ready?" My wife's green eyes lock onto mine as she asks, "What are you going to do with me, Robert?"

"You'll see, beautiful." I laugh a little as she giggles and I help her put her wrists into the handcuffs. Each one has a longer chain that a normal set, to allow Lauren a little movement, but it's important that she stays down during her encounter with the stranger. "I need you to wear this." I move toward her with the dark black, eyeless mask.

"Robert, I don't know," she says as she looks hesitantly at me. "We haven't done anything like this before, and I think you're going a little too fast for me. Maybe we can do this with the handcuffs but not the mask."

"No, you need the mask and some earbuds for your music," I reply as I reach toward her. "Trust me, Lauren. This is going to be a different experience that you'll enjoy."

"I don't know."

"Lauren," I scold. "Just do this for me, okay?" After some thought, my wife finally relents and nods her head. I slide the mask down onto her face and then place the earbuds into her ears before turning on the music. Taking a quick moment, I text downstairs to the man, "She's ready. Come up."

"OMW," he responds as I begin to rub Lauren's legs. I need to get this started so that when the other guy is here he can take over. As a matter of fact, he and I have already spoken by text a little about how things will have to work. I've told him what Lauren really likes in bed, especially as it concerns oral sex performed on her, and I've told him what brand of cologne I wear. I assume he will show up prepared, and as I go to the door I'm pleasantly surprised to see the young man waiting in clothing that is very similar to mine, a shirt and shorts.

"Come," I say quietly as I walk over to my wife. Lauren's legs are together, her knees bent as she lies on her back. She's waiting for whatever else I am going to do to her, and so I reach down and caress her long, soft legs slowly with my hands. The man stands and watches for a while to see how I move.

"That's nice, Robert," my wife moans a little as I run my hands from her legs to her feet. "Really nice." She gently opens her legs and I can see her bare pussy just underneath the nightie. "You know how I like it, baby, right?"

The man beside me looks at me for a moment before pulling off his tee shirt and shorts. His hard cock, a little longer than mine, springs free and it's obvious that he's happy to see my wife in person. "Let me," he says quietly. I back away and allow him to begin to caress Lauren's legs and feet.

"Quit teasing me," she says as she opens her legs wide, letting her knees drop to either side of her. "Oh, fuck, Rob."

The stranger runs his hands along the inside of my wife's legs slowly, goosebumps appearing on her as he moves up her thighs. He almost gets to her swollen pussy lips before reversing direction and moving back down her legs to her feet. I can see that Lauren is getting more excited each time he does this, at one point his fingers just barely brushing past her labia. *"Ohhh..."* My sexy wife smiles and wriggles around on the bed as if trying to force the stranger's fingers into her twat.

He looks at me and I nod, backing away to allow him room. I sit down at the small table to the side of the room and just watch, my cock as hard now as I think it has ever been. "Robert, I need more attention. You're going to make me explode if you don't take care of little sister." Lauren's *little sister* is her swollen clitoris that is now standing out just a little from her pussy lips. My wife has a meaty muff, and it's a pleasure on the tongue and lips to be certain. I watch as the stranger in our room slowly goes down on her and begins to nip and lap at her lady bits. "Fuck, Rob...*uhhh.*"

I pull at myself through my shorts until I free my own cock. I begin to stroke my penis as I watch the two of them together, my unknowing prude of a wife and the man who answered my advertisement at first to only trade nude pics of the women in our lives. As I think about it, what we're doing right now seems so odd. It's not what I had planned to do, but it's worked out so nicely at this point that I wish I had thought of trying it out sooner. "Oh, Rob," Lauren grunts as the stranger's tongue flits around her wet hole. "You're normally not so aggressive, honey." The man puts her legs back to better reach the entirety of my wife's valley and licks her from her tailbone and asshole to her clit. *"SHIT!"* my wife squeaks as her body shudders from the sudden pleasure of his muscular oral organ. "What the fuck, my love?" Lauren giggles as he does it again and again for a few times over. She likes it, even though her asshole is not normally a part of the body she will allow me to touch.

"Fuck me, Rob. Please fuck me." The man looks over at me and I nod again. He puts my wife's legs back and then pushes his large, hard pecker against her beaver. Lauren groans a little as he rubs his manhood against her wet slit, each time flicking her taut clit with the tip of his engorged, red penile head. "Holy *shit!*" Lauren grinds against his massive meat as he plays with her. The man doesn't have a condom on, but he's convinced me with a recent health check card to my text message box this morning that he is disease free and is willing to leave his jism on my wife's skin instead of inside her pussy. I'm allowing him to fuck her bareback as long as that condition is met.

His hard cock begins to slowly enter my wife's twat. "Rob, that's nice." Lauren always likes me to go in quickly because she has this belief that quick sex is the best sex. I'm surprised that she's okay with the slow tease the man is doing to her as he enters her. "What are you doing, honey?" The man pushes her legs back as he goes into her. "Easy, Rob, you know my cervix is low and not that deep. Easy. *EASY!*" As the stranger's cock finally seats deep inside my wife, he finds her cervix and wedges his cock against it. *"Shit, Rob...FUCK!"* Her toes point as he begins to thrust in and out of her wet hole. *"Deep, Rob, too fucking DEEP!"* The man's balls begin to slap her asshole as he pounds into her, my wife's lips pursed as he beats against the opening of her uterus.

"Rob, shit, what the fuck, honey?" Lauren's hands struggle against the handcuffs as she begins to grind beneath the man fucking her. "Damn, this feels good." I stroke my cock a little faster as I realize she's beginning to like what he's doing to her. "I think you're hitting my G-spot, Robert. You don't normally hit that for me. Keep going." Lauren bites her lip a little as he rams into her harder and harder, pushing her legs as far back as he can. I watch as my wife's sex juices roll down her slit and begin to wet the bed. My own pre-come is now lubricating my sex organ as I beat myself closer and closer to orgasm. "Rob, I'm going to come."

The stranger is getting closer as well, his face red as he begins to grunt and move around on top of her. Occasionally, he pushes himself all the way in and moves around as if stirring a pot with his cock, more than likely feeling the firm surface my wife's cervix provides. It really does feel good to roll the end of a cock along it, at least for a guy, but Lauren has often requested that I keep from going so deep to avoid doing that to her. It appears that now she's fine with it since he's stroking her G-spot so well. It's a trick that I'll need to remember if I want to have the same effect on her. *"Uhhh..."* The man looks at me. I'm close too and I can see what he wants. I nod my head to allow him to ejaculate into my wife's wet pussy. I'm so horny now that I don't care if he empties into her.

"Oh, Robert Jacob...*AHHHH!*" Lauren begins to orgasm as the man on top of her twists her nipples lightly. *"FUCK! ROB! FUCK!!!"* My wife is a verbal comer, and she lets loose in our hotel room as she grinds into the stranger's groin. *"Shit...OHHHH!!!"* Lauren's body tenses up and her back arches a little as the long pole of man meat continues to plunge into her lubricated snatch. *"Fuck me...FUCK ME!!!"* I worry that someone in another room might hear, but these newly renovated hotel rooms are supposed to have double the insulation of most hotels. Hopefully no one will hear my wife, but if they do I really don't care as I begin to feel myself going over the edge.

"Lauren," I moan as I begin to spurt into the air. *"Lauren..."* I'm not as loud as my wife as I attempt to be very careful about not letting on that I'm off to the side of the room instead of on top of her. I spurt hard into the air, my jism landing on my stomach and into the floor as I pop off, each one a bit of myself that I wish was going into Lauren's tight little vagina right now.

"Uhhhh..." The stranger comes into Lauren's ready and waiting pussy as he flexes his body. In and out, as if in some sort of rhythm, the man slaps his big balls against my wife. *"Gahhh..."* His spurts of man sauce must be powerful as he grunts and groans quietly on top of Lauren. She's his unknowing lover, her womb accepting his foreign seed as she comes with him. The idea that he's coming inside of her while she thinks it's me turns me on as I finish off my own orgasm. This is the sort of thing I'll beat off to in the future as I rehash this memory in my mind over and over again.

The man finishes off inside Lauren and then slowly pulls out of her. He nods at me as he pulls on his shorts and tee shirt before stepping to the door. As quickly as he appeared, the man is gone and I'm left to try to finish out the deception. After wiping myself off, I go up to Lauren and remove her earbuds and mask. Looking down at my wife, I ask, "Was that good?"

"Oh, *fuck,* Rob!" she replies with a giggle. "You've not been like that with me in...*forever!*" We laugh a little together as I reach down to take off her handcuffs. As I help my wife up, she sees the creamy, white deposit the man left rolling out of her muff. "You left me a lot to clean up," Lauren jokes.

"Yeah, sorry," I reply with a nervous chuckle. "I guess I got a little messy."

"I like it." My wife reaches down and dabs her finger into the jism at her slit. She then puts it to her mouth and takes a taste of it. "This is different. It's sweeter."

"Really?" I say as I sit down beside her. Is it possible for a woman to know the difference between semen taste?

"A little." She smiles. "You're eating more fruit in your diet. That must be it." Lauren smiles as she gets off the bed and heads to the bathroom to clean up. "Let's go out to celebrate the best fucking sex we've had in a long time, okay?" I nod as she closes the door.

"Fuck, Robert," I mumble to myself as I wipe my face with a hand. "Best fucking sex in a while." It's not the way I expected her to respond, but I suppose she's probably right in that assessment. We're not an overly sexualized couple, and at times we both ache for something more. Now that we've gotten that, my darling wife is certainly happy with the outcome. I just need to keep this secret about another man fucking her tonight; forever.

Chapter Four: The Wife

28

I like hot coffee. Maybe not as much as some, but I like the smell of it just before taking the first hot sip. However, I don't drink just any coffee that graces a cup in my hands. I like a special kind of coffee, primarily the type with far too much sugar and other flavorings. I have found the best coffee inspired caffeinated beverage is at one location in town, *Lou's Coffee Shoppe,* off the corner of Clearwater Avenue and Sixth Street. It's a good place to stop on the way to work, so today like so many other days I make my way into the small shop to get a caramel mocha concoction that would cause Willy Wonka to become diabetic. "Can I help you?" The barista smiles at me as she waits for my order.

I give it to her and then ask, "Can you add just a smidge of cream to it?"

"Of course, sir," she says with a smile. She's seen me in here so many times before that she doesn't even bother to ask my name, but writes *Larry* on the side of the cup. It's an inside joke of sorts, one that harkens back to about a year ago when she was going through a breakup with her boyfriend Larry. In order to try to lighten her somber mood that day, I had offered to be her *Larry* if I ever found myself without a wife. Ever since then, she has put his name on my cups as a way to commemorate the offer. Though, I've wondered since then, if she might actually be willing to let me be her boyfriend. She's very friendly to me, often a little flirtatious, but it might just be for the dollar or so tip I leave her when I get my coffee. Who knows? I don't really give it much thought.

"There you are," she says with a big smile as I pay her.

"Thank you. See you tomorrow." She nods at me before taking the next customer's order. As I turn I see a face that seems awfully familiar. Since I have a little extra time to spare this morning, I take a seat at a table no too far away from the familiar looking woman.

I watch as she sips her own coffee and looks at her cell phone. As I study her facial features, I'm certain that I know her, though my mind can't find a name to go with her face. Suddenly, she looks up and our eyes lock for just a moment before I look down at my own phone. My heart jumps as I open the downloads on my phone and look for a picture I received the other day. "Oh, fuck," I say under my breath. "It's her." The blue eyes and blonde hair are unmistakable. The man who fucked my wife two days ago sent me a picture of his wife, a full-frontal nude, that I found to be more than just a little sexually gratifying. I've jerked off to her image twice so far and I've even had a sex dream about her. In a town of more than two hundred thousand people, here she is just two tables away, in the flesh. I feel myself blush as I dare to raise my eyes to look at her again.

"Hello," I hear a voice say to the side of me. I turn and see the woman standing beside me. "Can I sit here?" My heart jumps as I nod slowly. What the fuck can I say to her? Does she know about me and about her husband screwing my wife?

"Um, I'm Robert," I say as I put a hand out to shake.

Taking it, she replies, "Mindy."

"Hello, Mindy." I gulp a little as she sits down across from me at the small table, her coffee in hand, before settling her eyes upon me. Feeling myself blush, I ask, "You come here often?"

Mindy smiles. "That's an old pickup line, Robert. You need to come up with a better one." She laughs a little before showing me her wedding band. "I'm attached, so you can relax. I'm not trying to pick you up." Her eyes settle on the wedding band on my ring finger before looking back up at me. "I just need to ask a couple of things if that's okay."

"Sure," I reply nervously.

"Do you know where Pensington Place is? I've got an appointment there for a job interview. It's at nine this morning, and I'm afraid that I'll miss it if I don't get on the right bus."

"Pensington?" I say with a smile. "That's close to where I work. As a matter of fact, I'll be heading that way in a few minutes and I can get you there if you don't mind a walk."

"Walk? It's that close?"

"Close?" I laugh a little. "Well, it's about four blocks, but it's easier to walk that distance than to wait for a bus or hail a taxi at this time of day. It's so busy that walking just seems to work out better."

"No car?" she inquires.

"Not for work. I leave it home unless I need to go further than work. Of course, if it's raining outside I might drive or even catch a bus." I scrunch my nose before adding, "The buses here, though, smell like urine. You should stay away from those if you can."

"Oh, understood," Mindy replies with a laugh. It's uncanny how much she looks like her picture, and I wish that I could be certain that she is the woman I have a nude photograph of on my phone. Of course, I could just ask about her tattoo near her bikini line, but I would be willing to bet that Mindy would not be so keen on my admission that I know of its existence. "So, you don't mind if a stranger walks with you?"

"Stranger?" I shake my head. "We're acquaintances now, so it's all good. We can walk together, though I won't quite accept candy from you yet." The two of us laugh a little more as we stand up from our seats. I turn and lead Mindy to the front door and open it for her, a whiff of her perfume filling my nostrils as she goes by me. The image on my phone continues to scroll through my mind as I imagine myself with her, naked and on top of her, my cock penetrating the small, tight, waxed pussy I've looked at dozens of times on my phone since getting it a few days ago.

"So, how long have you lived here in the city?" she asks.

"About eight years now, since getting hired with the bank where I work."

"Really? My husband and I just moved here last month. We're hoping to get a new start on things since..." Her voice trails off as she looks away. "Sorry, I'm getting a little too chatty. It's one of those little character flaws my husband dislikes."

"I don't see any character flaws," I tell her with a smile.

"You don't know me well enough." I feel myself blush again as I think about the nude picture of her I have just inside my pocket. I know a lot more about her than she could ever imagine. "I do talk too much."

"What's his name?"

"My husband?" I nod my head. "Tim. His name is Tim."

"What does Tim do for a living, if you don't mind my asking?"

She shakes her head as she looks straight ahead. I can see that Mindy struggles with an answer just before she replies, "He's got money. A little, anyway, since his mother passed away last year. She left him about three hundred thousand dollars and some property, but after taxes he's not got that much left. We've lived off some of it, and he's just blown some of it away. That's why I'm out looking for a job now and why he's going to work for a fitness place on the other side of town."

"He's a fitness trainer?" Mindy nods her head and I say, "Maybe I should meet this guy sometime and get some hints for getting rid of this." I pat my stomach a couple of times, causing my new friend to laugh a little. "Hey, the struggle is real," I say with a smirk.

"You look fine," Mindy quips with her own smile. "I'd go out with you." Her face almost instantly goes red as she quickly adds, "Like I said, I have a character flaw or two, and that was one of them. I tend to go way too far into making comments that are meant to be humorous and then realize that they're anything but."

"No, that's funny," I say with a smile. "I got it for what you meant it to be." My cock gets a little solid as I think about what it would be like to take the petite woman into my arms as I plant my penis deep inside her pussy. Mindy is shorter than my wife, maybe five-feet-two or a little less, and she can't weigh more than a hundred pounds. She's a spinner, and I'm sure the two of us could have loads of fun together. At least, we have in my imagination a couple of times as I've masturbated to her image on my phone.

"Anyway," Mindy continues while changing the topic, "I'm interviewing for a position with a law firm today."

"Law firm?" I suck a little air in as I think about my wife. "Which firm?"

Mindy smiles. "Greyson & Beck. They're looking for paralegals, and it so happens that I've worked in that capacity before. The position pays pretty well, from what information I've been able to gather, so I hope they'll like me enough to invite me to come work for them."

My heart flutters as I think about the law firm. My wife, an attorney for the past few years, works for Greyson & Beck on the other side of town. I was unfamiliar that they had another office near my workplace. "I thought they were located somewhere else."

"Apparently it's a satellite office that handles real estate issues and bankruptcies. It's separate from the larger office, but still a part of the same firm." I take a deep breath, hopeful that there will never be a way for Lauren and Mindy to meet. Of course, there really wouldn't be much of a danger in the two getting to know each other, provided I never see Mindy's husband again. We've seen each other's faces and that could prove to be pretty awkward.

"My wife works at the other site, handling corporate cases especially for one particular company just downtown. They have so much work for her, she practically lives at that company and only occasionally checks in with her bosses over at the firm."

"Very cool," the young woman says as we continue to walk. "We should all get together sometime. The two of you along with me and my husband. It would be fun." Mindy smiles, her blue eyes intoxicating as I look down at her. Would it be too inappropriate to try to bed her? I mean, Tim fucked *my* wife, right? It would be fair to fuck his wife in return, wouldn't it?

"Here we are," I finally say as I point toward the building where she says the satellite firm is located. "It's in there, but I'm not sure where since I didn't even know they had an office here." I take Mindy's hand again and say, "I always come through about the same time to get coffee. I wouldn't mind seeing you again and walking with you if you ever decide you want some company on the way to work."

"Sounds like a plan," she replies with a smile before turning to enter the building. "But I have to get the job first." Mindy waves and disappears into the entrance of the building as I try to tame the beastly hardon I've gotten while watching her walk away. I would fuck her, I'm certain of it, and I would fuck her in the presence of her husband if he wanted. Breathing hard, I continue for the next block to the bank just in time for its opening. The bank manager, an old golfing buddy of mine, gives me a funny look as I go inside. He knows I typically get here about ten minutes early, but today I'm almost late. Though I'm sure he wants to ask, he doesn't. In his mind, there's probably not an interesting excuse anyway. How little he knows of my suddenly interesting life.

Chapter Five: Something's Up

"Honey, what are you doing?" I look up from Lauren's pussy as her juices cover my face. "It's not the same as last week, Rob. Are you okay?"

I've tried to mimic what Tim did a while back for my wife, but I'm just not as good at it as he was. Lauren has noticed twice now that what he did for her and what I'm able to do for her now are two different things. As I look at her, I try to find an excuse that would be both acceptable and believable. "I guess it was the moment we were in at the hotel room, Lauren. I'm sorry that I am having trouble doing it exactly the same way for you again."

My wife's face shows her disappointment as she replies, "It's fine, dear. We all have our down times."

"You don't like this at all?" I kiss her swollen clit, a sign that she must be getting something from my attempt, hoping to elicit a favorable response.

"I like it," Lauren replies with an air or pity. "But it's just different, that's all."

"Sorry," I say with a bit of my own disappointment. I'm beginning to wish I had not allowed the other man with her at all. Had he been no better than me in bed, or even just a little bit worse, things would be a little different. Unfortunately, Tim is a man with talents that I cannot apparently call upon. He's good with his tongue and every other part of his body in ways that I just can't be right now. My oral work on Lauren sucks when compared to the way Tim nibbled her labia and clitoris, and it shows in the way my wife displays her disappointment.

"Maybe if I try the mask and the music?" she says with a hopeful tenor to her voice. "Maybe if we recreate it exactly as it was."

"Lauren, I don't know that I'll ever be able to do it that way again. I think it was a onetime thing that some guys have but never have again. Something took hold of me that night and I went crazy with you. I'll try to get it back, but please just keep in mind that there's no guarantee that I can ever do that exactly the same way again." I insert a finger into her wet pussy and begin to search for her G-spot. Lauren loves to have that stimulated, and when I do find it there seems to be consensus that she's having the best sex of her life. Unfortunately, as nervous as I am right now, I can't seem to find it.

"Rob, just stop." She reaches down and pulls my finger out of her wet hole. "It's getting irritated now. We've been at this for too long."

"We've been trying to have sex for less than fifteen minutes," I reply with a frown on my face. "Since when is that too long?"

"Oh, sweetie." Lauren always begins with exactly this condescending opening statement before launching into a lengthy dissertation of why most men are not good at sex. "It's not your fault. Men, in general, just don't sexually get it the way women do. They don't understand how to manipulate things down there in a way that pleases a woman the way a woman can please herself. It's rare that it happens exactly the way a woman wants, and most of us just put up with the shortcomings of our husbands and boyfriends, but in doing so we sometimes get irritated. I love you, but this isn't going anywhere." Lauren rolls over as she closes her legs. She's finished with me. I've taken longer than she likes to be involved in sex and when her decision has been made, it's final. Unlike her legal profession in a court of law, there are no appeals in the bedroom for me.

"That's not fair," I whimper as I sit up and wipe some of her drippings from my face. I know Lauren must have liked it at least to a point since she's so wet. However, she's a woman who wants it all or nothing. Now that she's experienced Tim, she wants what he can do for her, not me. The thing is, she has no fucking idea that it was another man who made her feel that way in the hotel room. As far as she's concerned, it was me, but a version of me she has decided to give up on experiencing this morning. "Nothing is good enough, is it?"

"What?" My wife looks over at me as she begins to get dressed for the day.

"No matter what I do, it will never be what you want in bed, Lauren. I try and I try, but you don't like what I do for you."

"I liked the hotel, Robert. If you could just do that..."

"I *can't* do that." I shake my head as I stand up from the bed, my penis growing softer as sex this morning becomes less likely. "I was lucky that night, and maybe a little different in the way I approached things, but you were different too. You were more patient, Lauren. You did something a little more daring than what you're used to and you were rewarded for it."

My wife frowns as she replies, "Look, we can't go back to the hotel right now, but maybe in a week or two..."

"Why can't we just fucking get off this morning? I would be willing to bet that we could just come and get it over with. I get so fucking frustrated when you just turn the tap off like this, Lauren."

"Turn the tap off?" My wife eyes me with a certain level of disgust as she looks me over. Lauren doesn't like having me challenge her in this way, as if to say that she is also somewhat sexually absent in the deal. She's great at throwing things off on me when it comes to the bedroom, but she really isn't able to take it as well as she dishes it out when we discuss our sexual desires and the lack of intimacy in our marriage. "Lay down, Robert."

"Why?"

"I'm going to get you off so you'll stop bitching about sex."

"Bitching?" I shake my head. "Get yourself off, Lauren. You need it more than I do."

"Robert, lay down or pack your fucking bags." I look at my wife and wonder why the hell she would level such a threat. There have been times when she has decided to just get me off, and to be honest her hand jobs are amazing, but she has never before said to me I had to choose between that or leaving the house.

"That's a stupid thing to say," I reply as I get onto the bed. "Really stupid."

"Sometimes you just don't listen." Lauren goes to the top drawer of her dresser and removes a small bottle of sex lube. I spread my legs and allow her to get in between them, the position I most enjoy when my wife is pulling on my meat. "Here." Lauren puts her bare feet on my balls and wiggles her toes to cause me to become fully erect again. I love her hand jobs, even when she gives them as a sort of consolation prize, but I can't seem to shake the intense dissatisfaction I feel as she puts a dab of the lubricant into both of her hands. Lauren first puts one hand over the head of my cock, causing my body to tense as the sensation of her slippery, small hand causes what feels like electricity to pulse throughout my body.

"Shit," I moan as she adds her second hand and begins to move up and down my shaft.

"There's nothing like a good old-fashioned hand job," Lauren says with a slight grin. "We'll work the tension out of you pretty quickly." My wife twists her hands a little as she goes up and down my cock, her toes wriggling on my ball sack.

"Oh, fuck, that's good," I moan as she uses a finger to press into the hole on the end of my phallus. Lauren has learned that I especially like having a fingertip pushed a little into my piss hole. The fact that it gets me off faster is probably the reason she employs the technique. My wife is all about speed and getting things done more so than the process of getting there for me. "I'm going to pop," I say as I grind into her feet.

"Good," she says with a smile. "I'm going to watch you spurt, Rob. Give me a couple of good ones, okay?" I nod enthusiastically as I get closer to releasing my seminal payload.

"Lauren, I let another man fuck you at the hotel," I blurt out as I get closer. I always get daring as I get close to an orgasm, and my wife has learned to ignore my outbursts. I've told her so many things about my hidden sex life, such as hiring a prostitute a couple of times when I've been away from home on a work trip, that she's come to not believe any of them. Of course, I normally recant the statement at the end of the orgasm, and she accepts that I'm just a talker. This time, though, I'm taking a real risk in sharing with Lauren the truth of what happened at the hotel.

"You did?" she says with a smile. "That explains a lot." I can tell by her expression and the way she continues to stroke my cock that she doesn't believe me.

"I really did," I groan as I strain to hold myself back from coming. "I let him lick you that way. It's why I can't do it again. Another man did that for you."

"Shit, Rob," Lauren replies with a smile. "You're really full of yourself this morning." My wife increases the rate at which she is pumping my penis.

"I shaved because he said I should. He said you might notice he was bald in the crotch if I didn't. Lauren, I really did let a guy fuck you." The daringness of my comment causes her to look into my eyes. Does she believe me? Is there some part of what I'm telling her that she could believe, even if I do generally lie during a hand job? "Lauren, he fucked you and I watched. It's why I had you wear the mask and earbuds…I…*UHHHH!!!*" I begin to spurt all over my wife's hands, and suddenly realize her pumping has slowed. Wrapping my hands around hers, I continue pulling up and down on myself with her soft skin still rubbing my cock. *"FUCK!! He FUCKED you!!! OHHHH!!!"* The look on my wife's face, the realization that I'm not lying, causes me to shoot hard as I move Lauren's hands up and down my penis. My ejaculation is powerful as I coat the two of us with more manly sauce that I've ever spilled before, and while I come I don't care if my wife knows. However, as I finish spurting, I begin to regret telling her. I finally release her hands and Lauren gets up quickly to go to the bathroom, where she locks the door.

"Honey, wait," I say as I get up from the bed and go to the door. "I was lying. You know how I am when I get off."

There's momentary silence before she responds, "You weren't lying Robert. I could see it in your face. You didn't fucking lie about this."

"Lauren," I huff as I put my head against the door. "Lauren, please, let's talk about this."

"I thought something was off," she says through the door. "You haven't been yourself since that night at the hotel and you've not done the same kind of things to me since then. I should have known. Maybe I did know and I just didn't want to accept it."

"Honey, please." What do I say now? I've fucked my marriage up because of a hand job and repressed sexual tension that I can't seem to ever get under control. "Lauren, I'm sorry. I shouldn't have done that to you."

"To me," she says from the other side. "That's how it happened. You did it to me without asking my permission." I can sense the attorney side of my wife coming out as she adds, "You could go to jail for this, Robert. What you've done is inexcusable."

My mind races with the thought of what my wife, the attorney, could, in fact, do to me. Lauren could take everything we own in a divorce and then simply charge me with some kind of crime. After all, I did let a man she doesn't know plow her muff without her approval. What kind of sick husband am I that I allowed that to happen? "Lauren, you can call the police or do whatever you want. Just open the door so that I can see that you're alright."

There's no response, so I turn and take a seat in a chair at the side of the room. Lauren has all the cards now and could play them however she sees fit. I'm an idiot. I've allowed another man to fuck her and then admitted it to her as I came into her hands. My sexual desires have gotten me in trouble, and I deserve whatever she decides to do to me. "Robert." I look up to see my wife standing at the doorway of the bathroom. "You're an asshole, sweetheart, but I've come to a conclusion. I want more of that night at the hotel."

"What?"

Lauren walks closer to me and asks, "What kind of guy was he? Was he at least attractive?"

Stunned by my wife's turnabout, I answer her, "He's a personal trainer, so he's in shape." I can see that Lauren is at least a little pleased by my answer. "Why?"

"I don't know," I answer. "I guess I just wanted to see you with someone else. There's really not much else I can say about something like that."

"Did you like it?" she asks. "Did it turn you on like you thought it would?"

"It was better than I expected," I answer as I feel my face turn red. "He was good at what he was doing and you were really into it. That got me pretty excited too."

"Did you get off while he was having sex with me?" I nod my head and my wife sits down on the end of the bed. "Do you think he would do it again?"

"Again?" I blink a couple of times as I consider her question. "I don't know. I would have to ask him."

"Is he a friend of yours? Maybe someone I know?"

"Neither," I reply. "I met him online when trading pictures." I bite my tongue as I realize I've just admitted to something else I should not have done.

"You sent him pictures of me?" Lauren looks down at her hands. "Was I naked in them?"

"Yeah," I reply softly. "I'm sorry, Lauren."

"Trading?" I nod. "Let me see."

"See?"

"What did he give you? Was it pics of his wife too?" Her eyes look up and meet mine for a moment. "I want to see what you got for mine, Robert." I reach over and retrieve my cell phone from the nightstand as my hand shakes. I pull up the one full-frontal image of Tim's wife that I have and hand the phone to Lauren. "Shit, honey."

"I'm sorry," I say with shame. "I shouldn't have done that."

My wife looks from the picture to me. "Do you like the way she looks? Does she turn you on?"

"I like it," I say frankly.

"Have you played with yourself while looking at it?" I nod my head as I look away. "Did you come while you looked at it?" I nod again. "Wow, honey. You'd fuck her if you could, wouldn't you?"

"Lauren, I…"

"It's okay," she quickly interrupts. "I understand."

"You do?" I prepare myself for the *but* that I feel is soon to come. My wife, a very capable attorney, can use and twist words in a way that's strangely appealing while also causing a measure of fear. She will probably use what she has on me now against me, and I have no one to blame for it all but myself.

"I want to fuck her husband again," Lauren says bluntly. "Can you send him a message or call him?"

"I could," I reply. "Would you really want to do it again?"

"Absolutely," Lauren says with a wicked grin. "Wouldn't you like to see that?" I nod and she hands me the phone. "Message him and let's see what we can do."

Looking at my phone, I open up a text message window with his number. After one last look at her, I send him a quick message asking if he would be game to have a repeat of the hotel meeting. I don't get a message for some time until a response finally pops up. "Sure."

"I think he's willing to do it," I tell my wife. "I mean, if that's what you want."

"Yeah," she says with a smile. "Without the mask and here at our house."

"What?" I look up and can see in her face that Lauren wants this badly. She wants to look into the eyes of the man who brought her to climax at the hotel and she wants to look into his eyes as she once again orgasms with him. "Whatever you want," I relent.

"And his wife?"

I shake my head. "No, not her. She isn't supposed to know either."

"I'll bet." Lauren considers this and says, "Tell him next weekend, okay? Maybe Saturday night?" I nod and send the message. To my wife's delight, he agrees and I give him the address. How strange it will be to have Lauren fucked by this stranger again, only this time while she knows it. How strange that she's not threatening to divorce me over this, but has embraced the idea of having sex with this man. I thought I knew my wife, but I apparently do not. We'll see what happens next weekend when Tim makes his way over to our home.

Chapter Six: She Can Never Know

"Good morning," I say to Mindy as I sit down across from her at the coffee shop table.

"Good morning to you too." She smiles at me warmly, her blue eyes studying my features as she takes a sip of her coffee. "What's the matter, Robert?"

"What? Oh, nothing."

"Nonsense. I've know you for what, two weeks? We've been walking together to work all that time and I think I've gotten to know you well enough that I can sense when something's not right. So, what's going on?" Mindy got the job as a paralegal at the law office where she applied, which I'm sure has been a huge relief for her and her husband financially. I have noticed in the short time that I've gotten to know her that Mindy is as astute mentally as Lauren. She misses very little in the way I look at her or behave, often asking questions that lead to some deeper truth with me. Mindy is never accusatory in doing so, unlike my lovely wife, but she is still very inquisitive when an opportunity presents itself.

"Things at home are a little off," I reply without being too specific. Her husband, Tim, is slated to appear in my bedroom tomorrow night to fuck my wife for the second time, this time with my wife's foreknowledge and without a mask. The idea that my new friend could discover her husband's unfaithfulness and my part in it causes a shiver to run the length of my spine. It also unsettles my stomach a little, which is why I have decided against coffee this morning.

"I'm sorry to hear that. Is there anything I can do to help?" It's a nice gesture, something one person might offer generically to another to show they do have a level of concern for another, but it settles in with me in a way that's less than socially acceptable. All I can think of is Mindy naked and in bed with me, satisfying me in a way that my wife never would.

I shake the thought and answer, "I appreciate that, but I think things just have to play out for now. My wife gets into moods and she just can't be talked out of something once she decides she's going to do it."

"I know what you mean," she replies. "Tim, my husband, is a bit of a determined guy as well." She leans close to me and adds, "I think he's having an affair, but I can't prove it."

My body shakes a little as I ask, "How do you know?"

Mindy's blue eyes focus on mine as she says, "He's going somewhere tomorrow night. He won't tell me where, but claims it's for a job prospect. I don't think he's being completely honest, though." She takes a sip of coffee and asks, "What do you think? Could my husband really be going out on a Saturday night just to look at a job or two? I mean, wouldn't most legitimate businesses interview or talk to you Monday through Friday and not on the weekend?"

"Not necessarily," I say as I try to find a way to alleviate her doubt in her husband. "He could be trying to get a job at a gym that's open twenty-four-seven. Sometimes those sorts of places have odd hours for interviews and tryouts."

"Yeah, I guess so," Mindy replies as she finishes her coffee. Turning our thoughts to other things, she says, "I wish you would have gotten a coffee too."

"Well, my stomach," I answer as I rub my belly. "It's a little soured this morning. Hopefully by lunch I'll be able to take something in."

"I hope so." Mindy smiles at me, causing my neck to bristle with tiny goosebumps as she gets ready to leave the coffee shop. There's a true concern on her part as it relates to me, which is nice when I consider what my relationship with my wife has become. "Come on, let's get going before we're both late." We laugh a little as I stand to my feet and we leave the shop.

"Chilly today," I say as I pull my jacket tightly around me. "Too damned chilly."

Mindy smiles. "It's getting colder now. I guess we'll start seeing snow pretty soon."

"Probably," I concur. "We get a lot of it here in the winter, but it seems like the weather is getting colder much earlier this year. We could be in for a tough winter by the time December gets here."

"Yeah, maybe so." Mindy wrings her hands together. "Here, I need to do something. Just don't freak out, okay?" She reaches over and takes my hand. Neither of us have gloves on, which has never been a problem for me in the fall, but her hand is ice-cold and I envelope it into mine. "Don't worry, your wife and my husband won't see us holding hands. I just need to warm up." Mindy looks up and smiles at me as I nervously smile back. Never before have I had a woman just put her hand into mine the way she has, and it unsettles me just a little. What if someone I know sees us together like this? How would I explain this away to my wife, that I'm holding the hand of the woman married to the guy Lauren will be fucking tomorrow night? I don't think her reaction would be as understanding as it was the other day when I told her about Tim. "Skin to skin is best to warm up, and people get so upset about something like holding hands."

I squeeze Mindy's hand tightly as I say, "It's a good thing we're not freezing to death out here. Then we would have to strip down and share body heat to stay alive." I chuckle a little as I look down. She blushes and looks away and I realize I've gone too far with it. "Just ignore me. I have the same problem with saying too much sometimes."

"No, it's not that," Mindy replies. "To be honest, I was thinking the same thing. It's just that..."

There's a silence for some time that I finally break by asking, "Just what?"

Mindy looks at me. "You're a nice guy, that's all. You're a *really* nice guy and you're not even complaining about holding my hand even though we are both married to other people. Someone like you comes along once in a lifetime, and sometimes that leads to confusing thoughts. I need to just shut my brain down and stop muddying the water."

"Muddying the water?" I study the way Mindy looks away from me and quickly understand what she's talking about. "Oh, my."

"I'm sorry." She drops my hand and puts the two of hers back together again as she tries to warm them. "Robert, I'm not being fair here, so please ignore me and my rants. I say too much sometimes. I just say too damned much."

I reach down and take her hand back into mine. We stop and look at each other on the side of the sidewalk as other people pass us by on their way to work. Looking into her eyes, I tell her, "I understand, Mindy, I really do. In a way, I agree with what you're thinking."

"Robert, I..." She reaches over and takes my other hand and for the first time I get to feel both of her hands at the same time. I can feel the warmth of my hands leave me quickly as the heat travels to her, and some part of me feels as if I'm transferring a small bit of my passion for her in the same way. Is it a certain level of love? That's impossible. I've only known her a couple of weeks now and something like that isn't so easily found. I love my wife, of that much I am certain, but confusion is beginning to trundle through my heart as I continue to look into Mindy's eyes.

"Let's agree that we like each other, okay? We're not signing divorce papers or telling our spouses to get out of our homes, just admitting that there's something between us right now. Maybe that will make things less of a problem for us."

Mindy looks down at the ground for a moment before looking back up at me. "I really like you a lot, Robert. A *whole* lot."

"I like you a whole lot too, Mindy. I'm going to go further to admit I have a strong attraction to you, and if I weren't a married man, I would..." Mindy suddenly reaches up and puts her hands on either side of my face to pull me close to her. Our lips meet and we both begin to nip, bite, and kiss at each other as if we've just discovered something magical between us. For what seems like eons, we continue to kiss as we embrace each other, our tongues finding their ways into each other's mouths as we explore what actually lies between us. There's no doubting now what we have. It's not just an infatuation or a passing interest. Mindy and I desperately want each other. We need each other.

"Shit," Mindy says as he pulls away from me. "Oh, I'm so sorry, Robert." The young woman backs away from me and begins to walk down the sidewalk quickly.

"Wait," I call out to her as I run toward her. "Did I do something?"

"Not you, me," she replies without turning around or stopping. "We can't do this again, Robert. We need to go our separate ways now."

"But, Mindy. I'm sorry for whatever I've done. Please slow down."

She turns and looks squarely into my face. "You don't understand. We are through with everything. I can't do this or…"

"Or, what?" I ask as I catch up with her. "What will happen?"

Mindy leans toward me and replies, "If we don't end this now, I'm going to have sex with you, okay? I will fuck you and I will try to take you from your wife. Neither one of us needs that on our conscience."

"But Mindy," I say as she turns and begins to walk away quickly.

"Don't follow me!" she squeals as she turns around briefly. Several other people stop and stare at me, causing me to freeze in my tracks. "It's over." Mindy turns and continues on her way.

A man stops and looks at me as he shakes his head and says, "Sorry, buddy. I've been there myself. Girls are tough that way." He then walks away and I feel myself begin to shake again.

"What the fuck have you done?" I ask myself as I put my head down. "What the fuck?" As Mindy gets further away, I begin to walk again. Today is a work day, regardless of my personal hurdles, and I'm almost late already.

Chapter Seven: My Wife's Desires

Our guest is early as he rings the doorbell. "He's here," I say when I see him through a window. Looking over at Lauren, I add, "I'll let him in." I get up from my seat on the sofa and walk over to the front door to let the man into our home. "Hello," I say as I offer my hand. He takes it and shakes it without saying much of anything before walking past me into the house.

Lauren comes to the door and looks at the man. "So, you're the one I have to thank for the hotel stay."

"My name is Tim," he says nervously as he offers his hand to her. "I'm sorry if I've caused you any worry over what happened."

"No, I'm past that," my wife replies as she takes his hand warmly. "Robert and I have talked about it a little and I felt it might be best if we get to know each other without the mask." She waves a hand toward the living room and we go inside.

"Tim, I know this is different than the last time, but Lauren found out that it wasn't me with her at the hotel, and she demanded to know about you. I guess you left an impression with her." I look over at my wife and can tell that she's fully enamored with the man. He's tall, maybe a little taller than me at over six feet in height, and weighs around two hundred pounds. Tim is physically imposing, his lean, muscular frame a bearing presence within the room as he sits down, although his personality not so much as he tends to avoid eye contact. He seems especially worried about the fact that his encounter with my wife is no longer a secret, considering that originally the secretive part was a piece of the plan.

"This is all new to me," he says as he looks at me and my wife. "I mean to say, that was the first time I've actually done something like that. It's not my normal way of behaving, but my marriage is just a little dry at this moment."

"Ours too," Lauren chimes in with a quick look at me. She leans toward the man and asks, "Did you enjoy being with me, Tim? Was it good for you?"

He smiles a little as he replies, "Yes, ma'am, it was really good. I guess I left the evidence of that with you."

Lauren giggles as she says, "Yeah, you left a *lot* of evidence inside of me. I'm just glad I wasn't ovulating."

"You have been on the pill for years," I interject as I look at my wife. "You were not going to get pregnant anyway."

"Still, you let a stranger get off inside of my vagina, Robert. That's not something most husbands would allow in the first place, especially without the woman's consent beforehand."

"I'm very sorry," Tim says as he adjusts his position in the chair. "I should not have suggested it." He looks over at me and adds, "We should have just kept it to pictures."

"The pictures," Lauren parrots as she sits back in her seat. "Did you like the ones my husband sent to you?" He nods as he looks at my wife briefly. "How many did he send?"

Tim looks at me and then back at her. "He sent about six, I believe. I sent him a couple of faceless ones, and then the one with her face."

"Your wife's face?" Lauren asks. Tim nods his head. "She's pretty." The man looks over at me with surprise before my wife adds, "I asked to see it. My husband admitted that things started out that way, but soon transitioned to where you fucked me in the hotel room." I can feel my cock get hard as I hear Lauren talk like this to Tim. "She's got a nice body. What kind of tattoo does she have down low?"

Tim clears his throat. "A leprechaun," he replies as his eyes shift from my wife to me for a moment.

"A leprechaun? That's an interesting choice." Lauren giggles a little as she asks, "Should I get a tattoo above my pussy too?"

"Lauren, what the fuck?" I chide her as I look over at Tim. "Don't mind her, she's in a mood today."

"I'm horny, Tim. Just fucking horny. My husband can't do what you do, so I wanted you to come over here and let him watch you with me again. I want you to make me come the way I did at the hotel that night and I want you to come as well. Only this time..."

"What?" Tim asks as he looks at her.

"I'm ovulating and I've not been on the pill in two weeks.

"You have got to be kidding," I say as I stare at my wife. "What are you up to, Lauren?"

"Russian roulette," she replies simply. "The kind that you can't simply die to get away from."

"No," I say emphatically. "We're not doing this."

"Oh, we're doing this," my wife says with a wicked smile crossing her face. "We're all in this now. Tim, would you like to fuck me again?" He looks at me and then back at her before he nods slightly. "Robert would like to see it too. I mean, look at the tent he's pitching in his pants."

"Lauren, I don't care if you want him to screw you again, but he has to cover his pecker."

"No, he's going bareback again. That is what you guys call it, right? Riding *bareback?*"

"Honey, this doesn't make any sense. Why would you want to take a chance that you could make a baby with a man you don't even know?" I look at a woman who is apparently still pissed that I've let another man fuck her the way I have, blindfolded and without warning that another man besides her husband would be using her sexually. I can understand her consternation, but I thought we had already gotten past this before Tim got here.

"So, here's the deal, Tim. I'm going to let things progress as far as the two of you allowed when you had sex with me while not wearing a condom. If I get pregnant, it's on you to provide half of the child support and my husband will provide the other half. However, if you refuse to have sex with me uncovered right now or if you ever refuse to pay for a child that could be produced, I'll tell your wife about your little foray into my pussy. And then I'll call the police."

"Shit," Tim says as he looks at me, his eyes wild with fear.

"Do it," I say as I nod toward him. "Just get it over with. We'll worry about something happening later, *if* it happens. We've never been able to have kids anyway."

"I'm ovulating, my love," Lauren reminds me. "I'm popping out an egg right now. My ovary is burning."

"Okay," I say as I put my hands into the air for a moment. *"Woo-hoo,* your ovary burns. Shit. Just fuck her and get this over with." I can feel a level of contempt for my wife. This is low even for her, but no lower than what Tim and I did at the hotel. I suppose we deserve this in a way.

"Let's do it," Tim says as he stands to his feet and pulls his shirt over his head.

"Whoa, cowboy. In here?" Lauren stands up as well.

"Yeah," he replies as he unfastens his belt and pulls his pants to the floor. His briefs show a tent being raised by his hardening cock as he looks at her.

"Fine." Lauren stands and begins to take her tee shirt and other clothing off as well. I watch as she unfastens her bra and her perky breasts pop out from behind it. Tim walks over after he finishes getting his underwear off and takes hold of one of my wife's breasts. "Tim," she moans as he fondles her hardening nipples.

"These are even nicer to see like this, while you are standing up." He bends down and takes one of her puffy nipples into his mouth. Tim begins to lick and suck her milk mound as Lauren puts her hands on his head. My wife loves to have her nipples sucked, and I think it's one thing that I actually do very well when it comes to making love to her.

"Oh, Tim. Hang on." My wife pulls away so that she can get her blue jeans and thong underwear down. Her soft, hairless muff glistens with her own dew as she stands in front of her lover. "Touch me," she begs as she pulls in tightly to him again. Tim reaches down and fingers her soft, tight snapper, causing my wife to put her head against his shoulder and begin to moan. *"Oh, shit…"*

"Do you like that?" I ask as I watch the two of them together, the man's fingers inside of her.

"I love it," my wife replies without looking back at me. "I fucking love it." She pulls Tim's head to hers and begins to kiss him deeply as he continues to fondle her pussy.

"Fuck!" Lauren grips Tim's large penis while she's kissing him, causing him to become fully aroused. "I didn't get to feel your hand on it last time, you know." He smiles at her as she pulls at his meat. "This is really nice." Lauren then bends forward and begins to lick his nipples as she handles him manhood.

"Shit, wife," I say as I pull my own cock out of my pants. "I mean, fucking *shit…*"

Lauren looks over at me. "This is what you want, right? You want me to fuck Tim and to let him come inside of me, even if I could get pregnant?"

As I tug at my own pecker, I reply, "It's the fact that he could get you pregnant that turns me on like this," I admit as I get a little pre-come to spill from the tip of my penis. Using it to lube the head, I begin to twirl my fingers over the tip of my johnson as I add, "You like it too, though. You must, or else you wouldn't be doing this right now."

"Yeah," she replies. "I really like it." Lauren sits back on the sofa just a few feet from me and Tim pulls her legs back. He begins to lick and lap at her long crack again, just as he did at the hotel, beginning with her puckered asshole and ending with her swelling lady bit. "Tim, that's really nice. Keep doing that, sweetie." The young man pushes his face into her wet muff, hungrily going after my wife's sweet taste as he pleasures her.

"I'm going to fuck you hard," he promises as he lifts up from her. "Really hard." Tim pushes his large cock against Lauren's wet hole and pushes into her. "You're fucking soft and wet."

"Oh, shit," my wife moans as he parts her pussy lips. I stroke myself hard as I watch his first penetrating thrust into her, causing Lauren to tense and point her toes when he finds her cervix. *"Fuck!"* Tim's balls slap her asshole hard as he pushes her legs back and continues to fuck her hard, just as promised. *"EASY, Tim...FUCK!"* He feels her cervix now, low and hard, ready for his man sauce as he plows my wife's fertile field. The young man wants her badly, and he'll have her the way he wants her.

Tim suddenly pulls out and lifts Lauren from the sofa, not a difficult thing to do considering she's so lightweight. "Over," he grunts as he helps her up before bending her over the arm of the soft, leather furniture.

"What are you doing?" Lauren asks as she looks back at him. "Doggy style?"

"Yes," Tim responds as he spits on his hand and rubs his penis. "Over." He pushes my wife down and presses his large member against her tightly puckered asshole.

"Oh, shit, *no anal!*" Lauren pleads as he presses forward. My wife isn't a huge fan of ass fucking, but I can see that Tim wants to feel her tight sphincter around his swollen manhood. What man wouldn't? My wife's ass is soft and tight, something that she's only allowed me to feel once and not to completion.

"Yes," he moans as he pushes into her ass.

"Tim, don't," my wife says as she looks back at him. The young man simply puts his hand on her head and pushes her back down as he enters her ass. "Oh, *fuck!*" I watch as his pecker sinks slowly into Lauren's tight asshole, my wife gripping the leather on the sofa tightly as she grits her teeth and tries to take it in without freaking out.

"I wish I was doing that," I say as I watch his cock finally disappear into her back door. "Fuck, I wish I could do that with you." Lauren only opens her eyes for a moment to look at me, but closes them again as Tim begins to thrust in and out of her ass. "Is she tight?"

Red-faced, the young man turns to me and says, "She's so fucking tight I can barely stand it." He's getting close to losing his load and I can feel mine working its way up as well as I stroke my man meat. "Lauren, I'm going to come in your ass."

"Shit," she moans as she moves her hand over the arm of the sofa and between her legs. She begins to twirl her clitoris furiously with her fingers as she begins to enjoy the feeling of Tim in her asshole. "Oh, Tim...*uhhhh...*"

I pull at myself faster and faster as I begin to teeter on the edge of an explosive orgasm. I want to shoot off, and I want to make a mess while doing it. Some part of me wonders whether I could get any of it to land several feet away on my wife's back, though I doubt that. But it would be nice if I could.

"Oh, Tim, *uhhhh!!!*" My wife's small body suddenly begins to rock around over the sofa arm as she goes into full orgasm. *"Ohhh!!! SHIT!!!"* Lauren grinds her ass into Tim's groin, his hardness moving in and out of her so fast now that he might tear her apart. His balls are slapping her and the sofa arm beneath her so hard that I believe one or both of the lovers will be bruised from the constant impacts. All Tim wants right now is to blow his load into my wife, and all she wants is to take it all into her anal void. *"Come in me...COME IN ME!!!"* Lauren shrieks as her body continues to have wave after wave of orgasmic energy pass through it.

"I'm *coming!!!*" Tim begins to shoot his load into my wife's ass, humping her so hard now that he almost tosses her off the sofa arm. *"Uhhhh...OHHHH..."* I stand to my feet as I feel my own jism coming up to explode as well as I watch the two lovers enjoying each other. *"Ahhh...mmmm!!!"* Tim watches me as I step close to my wife's head.

I reach down and pick up Lauren's head and turn her face toward me. Pressing my cock against her lips, I push in and almost immediately begin to squirt. "Swallow it...*swallow!*" I spurt hard and fast into my wife's throat as Tim continues to dump his load in her ass, each of my ejaculates making her gag as I force my cock deep into her throat. *"Ohhh...FUCK!!! SWALLOW, Lauren...SWALLOW!!!"* There's something about having a woman take you in and gulp down your semen, and I have missed having that with my wife. I like having Lauren blow me and downing my white man sauce, but it's something she normally refuses to do. Today, though, I get to enjoy feeding it to her. *"Uhhhh..."*

Tim pulls out as I finish off in Lauren's mouth. "Shit," he says as he sits back on a chair as his cock begins to wilt.

I pull my phallus out of my wife's mouth and allow her to relax over the arm as she coughs with my jism rolling out of the corner of her mouth. There was a lot of jism that came out of me, and I know she swallowed at least some of it, though Lauren certainly doesn't seem all that happy about it. "Thank you, honey," I say with a wicked grin on my face.

"This was supposed to be between just Tim and I," Lauren growls as she stands up from the sofa arm. "You were supposed to stay back and just watch, Robert."

"Okay," I reply as I sit back in a chair. "I just wanted to enjoy my wife today as well. What harm is there in doing that?"

"What harm?" Lauren glares at me as she walks up to me. "This was supposed to be a repeat of the hotel incident. You were supposed to stay back and let me have a little fun with him, not with you." She glares over at Tim. "You let him come in my mouth."

"Um, what could I do? I was getting off already and he's your husband. What would you have had me to do? Pull out and get into a fight?" The young man seems as perplexed as I am about why Lauren is so miffed about what happened.

"Shit," she moans as she sits down on the sofa. "Not next time, though," she warns me as she looks up. "Next time it's just the two of us." Lauren motions toward Tim as she stares at me. "Just us."

"Next time?" Tim says as he looks over at my wife. "Really?"

"I want more of you," she answers quickly. "Without my husband interfering. Right, Robert?" Lauren waits for me to respond, and all I can do is nod my head. I suppose that I'll have to sit back to allow that when it comes time, considering I'm the one who started all of this.

"When?" Tim asks with an air of excitement about him.

"Next weekend," my wife replies. "Over here again." He nods and looks over at me. I can see that he wants some sort of understanding from me before he decides to actually take Lauren up on the offer. "No, he's not the one deciding this," she adds. "Here, next weekend, same time." It almost sounds like a directive from a supervisor at work, a person not to be trifled with. Tim quickly relents and nods before getting up to put his clothes on. I gather mine up and leave the living room to go to the bathroom.

"Wow," I say to myself as I shake my head and close the bathroom door. "You have gone off the deep end, my love." Lauren has always been headstrong, and it appears she is just as headstrong about this as she has been about anything else. What Lauren wants Lauren gets. There's not much I can do at this point to stop her.

Chapter Eight: A Friend's Request

"Mindy," I say as I approach her from behind. She stops and turns to look at me as I catch up to her.

"Robert," she says sullenly. "We can't do this."

"Do what?" I ask with a smile. "I just want to see how everything is going for you, that's all." It's been two weeks since the young woman broke off our friendship. Her feelings for me, and quite probably my feelings for her, were beginning to be a problem for the two of us. Mindy was the first to understand where things were going if we didn't do something, and she was the only one of us to be adult enough to break things off before they got started. I can see in her face that my approaching her today has brought back some pain.

"It's too much," Mindy says as she begins to shake a little. "Just too much."

"What's too much?" I reach out to touch her arm, but she pulls back to avoid allowing me to make contact. "Mindy, please. What's going on?"

"Tim," she laments as she turns and begins to walk again. I follow right along beside her as I wait for further explanation. "He's *really* into another woman."

"He's told you this?" My heart thumps inside my chest as I look down at her. He's been with my wife twice more since Lauren let him fuck her at our house the first time, and both times they've gone off to the bedroom and locked me out. She doesn't want me to watch anymore, probably because she's afraid that my sexual desire will push hers to the side when at the height of climax. Lauren is insistent, though, that if I allow this to continue she will *take care of me* and my sexual needs later. It's a promise that I'm not certain she plans to fulfill anytime soon.

"He goes somewhere every Saturday evening." Mindy wipes a tear from one of her eyes. "I know he's up to something, though. Tim doesn't have any drinking buddies or bowling buddies. I've been checking around, and I can't find anyone my husband knows who is going out with him. It has got to be a woman, Robert. I just know it." I ache to tell her. Just to level what I know with her would be a great burden lifted from me, but one that would more than likely be the complete end to our friendship. How would I go about telling her that I'm basically allowing her husband to have sex with Lauren? Worse yet, how would I explain that I *invited* him to take my wife the first time around? What sort of person would such an admission make me out to be in the eyes of the young woman walking beside me?

"You can't be certain of what he's doing, Mindy. Maybe you're just letting your imagination run wild? I mean, look at you. You're a beautiful woman that any man would be lucky to call his own."

Mindy stops and looks over at me. "This is why I can't be around you, Robert. You're too damned sweet to me and it causes me to think things that I really shouldn't." She turns her head and continues to walk as I stay beside her.

"I'm sorry," I say after a minute or two of silence. "I guess I can't help but to be honest with you. You're a beautiful young woman in the prime of your life and you deserve better. I mean, if you can't trust the man, why stay with him?"

"Do you trust your wife, Robert?" Mindy asks bluntly without looking at me. "Do you really, *really* trust her? Or are there things that she does that causes you to doubt her just a little bit?" It's a cutting question that I really don't want to answer. Of course I can't trust Lauren. She's proven over the past couple of weeks that she is willing to be very active in a sexual relationship with another man and to do so in our home without allowing me to watch. The times she has had him over are the times I *know* about and don't include the evenings when she comes home late. I've been a little suspicious of her activities recently, but haven't really dwelt on those suspicions until now.

"I'm not sure," I say with a huff. "Not really sure at all. Then again, I think sometimes jealousy and bitterness creep into relationships.

Sometimes they don't amount to much and sometimes they do. I think maybe you and I are kindred spirits in a way here.

Mindy stops and turns toward me. "I need to take you somewhere, okay?" I nod and the young woman takes me by the hand to lead me down a street where we don't usually walk to go home. For fifteen minutes we walk hard, her hand squeezing mine tightly as I think about how soft her hand is in mine. Lauren's hands are soft too, but there is something different with Mindy's hands. They're almost frail, as if close to a heartbreak that could end her. I'm falling for this woman, and I'm not sure that I can keep from professing such feelings to her if the opportunity were to present itself.

"Here," she says finally as she points to a small place called *Copper Pig Tavern* along the sidewalk. I've not been here before, but it appears to be a very quaint location surrounded by larger, more modern shops and restaurants. "I'll buy you dinner, okay?" Her eyes only hold mine for a moment before she leads me through the door.

"Wow," I say as we go inside. The theme of the place is very much old-world with wood slat tables and seats lit by dancing flames of faux-flamed candles. The rustic ambiance of the establishment is highlighted with servers that appear in serving wench outfits that highlight their bust lines, a bit of blush set upon their cheeks to finish out the look. I would have never thought that such a place existed in the city, but here it is, a few customers scattered throughout.

"Would you like a table?" a woman asks. Her eyes then widen as she looks at Mindy. "Hey! How have you been, Min-Min?"

"Min-Min?" I repeat as I watch the two women hug each other.

Mindy smiles as she looks at me. "This is Janey, an old friend of mine. Janey, this is Robert."

"Um, this guy isn't Tim." An accusatory look comes across the server's face as she looks me over.

"A friend," Mindy replies with a grin. "I just want to show him the place and maybe get a bite to eat if we could. Maybe in my old spot?"

"Sure," Janey replies with a faint smile as she glares at me. "Follow me." Mindy and I walk right behind her as she leads us to a table in a corner, one that is a bit darker than most other parts of the tavern. "Here you go," she says as she places menus on the table. "I'll have someone over to take your order in a bit." The server has one last look at me before walking away.

"She doesn't like me," I say as I look at Mindy. "Let me guess; she knows Tim pretty well."

Mindy nods before replying, "She's his cousin. I worked with her here for a couple of years and she was the one who introduced me to my husband. She ended up being one of my bridesmaids at the wedding as well."

"Oh, wow." I look over at the woman and notice her staring in our direction. "Okay, so tell me, Mindy. Why are we here?"

"Dinner," she says with a smile. "Just a bite to eat. I had a light lunch and I'm famished."

I shake my head. "No, really. Why are we *here*. There are maybe a dozen restaurants along the way to the coffee shop and you decided to turn the corner and walk two blocks to this tavern. What's going on?"

"Nostalgia," Mindy answers directly as she focuses her blue eyes on me. "I haven't been here in a long time, so I wanted to come here. You're welcome to leave if you want to, though," she tells me as she looks down at her menu.

Mindy is rarely so coarse with me, which causes me to become quiet for a while. I look over the menu as well for some time before a different server comes up to us and takes our food and drink orders. I'm not hungry, so I don't order a heavy meal, just an appetizer. Mindy does the same, and we agree to split them with each other. Once the food arrives, we eat and talk a little, the subject of our conversations not worth much as we dine together. Something is up with Mindy, but I can't put my finger on it. Her mind is preoccupied and the look on Janey's face from a distance continues to vex me as I see her out of the corner of my eye. The woman doesn't trust me, and maybe she shouldn't. After all, my thoughts concerning Mindy are deep today and I can't seem to bring myself around to quelling a single one of them.

"Finished?" a server asks as she walks up.

"Yes, thank you," Mindy says as the woman begins to remove our plates. We sit for a moment after she leaves before Mindy looks up at me and asks, "Would your wife miss you tonight if you didn't come home?"

"Miss me?" I look over at her as my heart races. "Mindy, what are you saying?"

"Would she miss you if you told her you would be working late? Or staying out?" I can't avoid her sharp gaze, Mindy's eyes looking through me in a way that it feels as if she's studying my soul.

"I don't know," I reply honestly. It's not something I've given much thought to. My work rarely requires late hours, considering that banks are institutions given to service hours that end earlier than most other jobs.

Mindy looks over at another server, and after their eyes connect the server walks over to our table. Mindy asks, "Is the upstairs still available?"

The woman looks at me and then back at Mindy. "Yeah, we can do that. But Janey..."

"Not a word to her," Mindy says quickly as she looks up at the woman. "Can you do that for me? Book it?"

"I can, but you have to know that not much happens here without Janey knowing about it. She'll blab it to Tim."

"Let her blab," Mindy replies with a scowl on her face. "I just need the room for me anyway."

"Okay," the server replies as she looks over at Janey. "I'll make the booking in the office where she won't see me do it."

"Thanks, Sue." Mindy watches the woman leave before asking, "Will you do something for me?"

"Anything," I respond after clearing my throat. "Leave the tavern and then wait until I text you. Come back in immediately after my text, okay? Don't wait too long to do it or it will spoil everything." Mindy gestures over toward a door at the back. "Then come straight back to there and after you go through the door turn right. Go up the stairs to the room I've given you in the text."

"Room?"

"There are three up there that they let out once in a while. I wasn't sure whether they still do it, but apparently, they do. Knock on the door three times and I'll let you in."

"Mindy," I begin as my voice shakes.

"I need this favor, Robert. Just do this one thing for me and then you can leave. I promise, I'm not asking for sex. Okay?" I nod and Mindy looks over at Janey. "Leave now so that she can see you, but stay close for my text. You'll have a window of maybe five minutes to get back here."

"Alright," I answer with confusion filling my mind. What could she be up to? Why rent a room out for the night and not want sex? I get up from the table and make my way toward the front of the tavern, where I make certain to nod at Janey and say, "This was a very nice place. Thank you for the meal."

"Anytime, sweetie," she says with a limp grin on her face. She really doesn't like me, and I'm certain that it has everything to do with Tim. I walk out the door and go down to a small electronics store to browse the items on the shelves as I await Mindy's text message.

Chapter Nine: What's Not the Matter

My cell phone buzzes in my pocket. I reach into my pocket to pull it out and read the message. "Come now." Turning for the door of the small electronics store, I walk back out to the sidewalk and straight to the tavern. I cautiously enter the front door and see no one at the front kiosk. Janey is nowhere to be seen, and so I make my way to the door where Mindy instructed me to go earlier. Turning right, I walk up the old wooden stairs and look at my phone again for a second text message. "#3." I look around at the three old wood panel doors and find the one with a brass 3 on the front. Knocking three times, I look around as I wait for Mindy to open the door.

"Hey," she says quietly as she opens the door. "Come in." I walk past her and she closes the door behind me. "We have to be quiet," Mindy tells me as she directs me to a chair on one side of the small room. I look over at the full-size bed and other room accoutrements and wonder how many people stay here over the course of a week. There's not a sign on the front of the tavern advertising rooms, so there would be no way for the average person to know they could request lodging. It makes everything about this a little stranger.

"So, why are we here, Mindy?" I ask as I settle into the seat.

She shakes a little as she looks at her hands. "I need to know something."

"Know something?" I chuckle a little. "Like what?"

Mindy's jacket is already lying over the back of a chair nearby, as her hands begin to fiddle with the buttons of her blouse. "I need to know what you think of me. I need to know that it's not me that's the problem in my marriage."

"Mindy?" She opens her blouse and shows me her slight cleavage behind a crème-colored bra.

"I know I'm small," she mumbles as her blouse goes to the floor and she begins to unfasten her bra. "I just need to know if you think this is what's driving him away." Mindy drops the bra to the bed and her small,

B-cup breasts stiffly point toward me, the pink color of each one much more vivid than in the pictures Tim sent me more than a month ago.

"Mindy, this is so weird." My eyes look from her chest to her eyes. I try to keep my growing bulge from her sight as I look at her topless form.

"Are they disappointing?" she asks me as she walks up to my chair. "Is this something you would want your wife to fix if she had boobs this small?"

I shake my head as she gets within inches of my face. "They're perfect," I blurt out. "They're better than any I've seen before. You should be proud of them." The puffy nipples of her mammaries cause me to yearn for the woman standing in front of me right now. I want Mindy, but I know to have her would be to risk double jeopardy.

"Touch them," she pleads as she reaches for my hands. "Just hold them and tell me how they feel." Mindy takes hold of my hands and pulls them up to her chest. Placing my hands on her breasts, she says, "Squeeze them and touch them however you want. Then give me your honest opinion, okay?"

I nod and do as she asks, feeling the firmness of each as I gently cup them and play with them. Mindy's nipples harden reflexively as my fingers slide past them and I begin to wish I could open my pants and take her on the bed right now. "Mindy, they're really nice. I don't know what else to tell you, though. I like breasts this size that feel this way, so I'm biased."

"Most guys like big ones," she laments. "Tim likes them a little bigger too."

Looking up at her, I reply, "He asked you to change them, didn't he?" She nods her head as a tear comes to her eyes. "Don't do it."

"Don't?" Mindy wipes her eyes and says, "If I don't, he might stop finding me attractive. He might go after another woman." My heart aches as she talks about another woman, given that I know exactly who the other woman happens to be. "What about this?" Mindy pulls down her skirt and underwear as she shows me the rest of her body. "I did this for him, and it seemed at the time to really turn him on." She points at the small tattoo of a leprechaun above her bikini line. "This was for him and it made him happy."

I can smell her warm snatch as I look closely at the tattoo that I've already seen in a picture of her naked body. "You're beautiful," I catch myself saying again as I look at her bare hooch. I want to touch it, to see how soft her thin labia and small clitoris happen to be, but I don't dare do it. She's not my wife, and though I've allowed Lauren to play, I've convinced myself that I will not.

"Robert," Mindy says softly as she puts her hands on the sides of me face. "Would I be too forward to ask to see you with your clothes off?"

"I can't," I say quickly as I look at her.

"You can't?" I can tell there's some disappointment in her voice, which causes me a level of disappointment in myself. If I take off my clothes or even stand to my feet, Mindy will see how excited I am to see her naked. I'm not sure that would be a good idea.

"I want to compare." She smiles at me. "I want to see what you have that might be like his, or even different. I've not been with that many men, so I'm curious." Mindy strokes the sides of my face as her pussy essence continues to fill my nostrils.

"I'm embarrassed," I reply as I look up at the young woman again. "I don't know if I want you to see me naked."

"Are you aroused?" Mindy guesses my reason for modesty and I look down at her feet. They are such nice-looking feet and I want to feel them on my cheeks as I bury my cock deep inside of her.

"I guess," I awkwardly reply. "Maybe a bit too much."

"It's okay." Mindy takes my hand and helps me up from the chair I've been sitting in. "You're bulging."

"Yeah," I reply as I blush. "I'm sorry if I'm offending you. I know you just wanted my opinion, and instead I'm offering you a crude bodily function."

She giggles a little before replying, "It's the highest form of compliment." Mindy reaches over to me and begins to loosen my necktie. "Do I need to help you?" Her blue eyes meet mine and I nearly melt beneath her gaze. My hands move to the top of my shirt as she removes my tie, and I begin to unbutton it. Mindy backs up and watches me disrobe, everything coming off over the course of a couple of minutes, until I get to my white briefs.

"I'm sorry," I say again as I pull them down to reveal a very stiff penis to her.

"Don't be," Mindy replies softly as she looks at me. "You're handsome, Robert. You have a very nice body. Even that." The young woman points at my hard manhood as she continues to smile at me. "Do you want me, Robert?"

"Yes," I answer meekly. "I want you very much, but we're married."

"It doesn't matter now, does it? I mean, your wife and my husband are getting along nicely."

"What?" I take a deep breath as if I've just jumped into an ice-cold lake. "What do you mean by that?"

"You know what I mean," Mindy replies as she walks up to me. I can smell the perfume on her neck as she gets close enough to me that my pre-coming dick leaves a wet spot on her stomach. "I've seen your wife's pictures and she's beautiful."

"Shit," I reply as I begin to feel as if I might throw up. "I'm sorry, Mindy. This has all gotten out of hand."

"She's not the first," the young woman tells me as she reaches out and takes hold of my male member. Tugging at it gently, she explains, "Tim has been meeting up with women for the past couple of years. He doesn't know it, but I've been keeping tabs on everything he's doing. Just like he keeps tabs on me."

"Janey," I grunt as she pulls on me.

"Yeah, she's his little spy. Each time he's found a woman, he goes and does what he does until he's tired of them. Then he comes back to me. The only problem is, I'm not doing that anymore. I'm not taking him back."

"I'm so sorry. It's all my fault. I let him do things with my wife..."

"I know," Mindy replies as she kisses my chest. "I've known the whole time. Brent tells me everything."

"Brent?"

"Tim's brother. The thing is, my husband talks incessantly to his twin brother to the point that he shares everything that he does sexually. Brent, who feels a little bit of loyalty to me, tells me about them. He even had Tim send the pictures of your wife and your messages to him. He told his brother that it was his own personal fetish to know what Tim was doing with other women. So, my husband freely shares that with him."

"You've known the whole time?"

"I have, but I've never lied to you. I've never been dishonest with you at all, Robert. I know what that's like, and I didn't want to take you from Lauren because I know Tim will tire of her soon and she'll need you."

"Even that first time at the coffee shop? You *knew?*" Mindy nods her head as she keeps stroking my penis slowly with her two soft hands. My mind, though occupied heavily with what she's doing to my crotch, begins to formulate what exactly has been going on. Everything we've talked about, everything we've done, has had a glaring presence of which I was unaware. "You hunted me down to see who I am, didn't you?"

"I saw you after I found out about your wife. It was then I decided I needed to see you and just have a face to put with the woman my husband is fucking. I wasn't going to talk to you in the coffee shop, only watch you for a few, but then you sat down. You weren't supposed to do that, but you were supposed to leave and then I would have gone on and never met you. Your actions caused me to want to meet you, and since that time I can't get you out of my mind. I'm falling for you, Robert."

Mindy lowers herself to her knees and pushes my cock into her mouth before I can say anything to her. Her soft, thin lips wrap tightly around my thick manhood as she pushes it to the back of her throat, gagging a little as she deepthroats me in a way that my wife has rarely done for me. "Shit, Mindy," I moan as she puts a hand on my balls and begins to fondle them lightly. "Oh, hell, why are you doing this? I'm not even as good looking at your husband. I'm not a guy half as nice as what a woman like you can have."

She stops sucking on me and looks up with a smile. "You've listened to me and been a good friend, Robert. You've given me more attention in a month's time than Tim has given me in several years of marriage. You're the real deal when it comes to a man, not my husband. I want *you,* Robert, not Tim." Mindy draws me back into her mouth again and continues to suck on me as I put my hands on her head. She knows what she's doing, her tongue sliding from the end of my cock to my ball sack as she blows me, causing me to become harder than I have been in years. It won't take much to bring me to an explosive conclusion.

"Oh, Mindy, I'll come if you keep going," I tell her as she bobs on my phallus. "Ooh, fuck."

"Lie down," is her response as she stands up and takes my hand. "On the bed. Lie on your back." I don't question what's about to happen, but I lie down and Mindy follows me to the bed. Again, her lips slide over my hard penis for a moment before she swings a leg over me and positions her wet hole just over my cock.

"I don't have a condom," I say to her as Mindy begins to put me into her vagina. "I can't keep myself from coming. I'll probably come pretty quickly."

"You don't need one with me," she replies without offering an explanation. Is Mindy infertile in some way? Or does she simply mean she's disease free? Either way, I don't care as I feel her moist softness begin to surround my cock.

"Fuck," I moan as she sits completely down on me.

"You're fucking long," Mindy moans as she leans back and begins to go up and down on my pole. "Really fucking long."

"Mindy." I reach up and cup her small breasts again, pinching her nipples lightly as she works herself up and down on me. Just now, I'm doubtful the young woman weighs even one hundred pounds as she goes up and down. I've never had a lover as petite as her, and my mind allows thoughts concerning whether I could spin her on top of me. Those thoughts disappear as Mindy puts a hand on her swelling clitoris.

"You rub me just right," she groans as she plays with her clit while going up and down on me. "I want you, Robert. *Fuck,* I need you." The small woman begins to rock faster and faster on me as we both approach an orgasm.

"Mindy, holy hell." My body begins to flex as I feel myself getting closer to coming. Just now, I can't wait to fill her hole with my semen. I want to know that some small part of me is a part of her.

"Robert, I'm coming," Mindy growls as she rocks me and the bed around. I'm sure by now that someone must hear the loud creaking of the bed frame. "Oh, Robert...Rob...*uhhh...OHHHH...AHHHH!!!*" Mindy convulses into an orgasm as she squeals loudly on top of me. *"Ohhh...uhhhh...FUCK!!! FUCK!!!"* My wife can be vocal, but I think Mindy absolutely wins out in her verbalization of sexual climax. *"Gahhh...mmmmm..."*

"Shit!" My body suddenly thrusts upward, almost bucking Mindy off me as I begin to spurt my seed into her womb. *"Mindy...SHIT!"* I grab onto her and slap my balls against her ass as I push in and out of her as I come inside of Mindy's pussy. Her soft, tight snatch feels so much nicer that Lauren's as I leave my jism inside of her. *"Ohhh...AHHH!!!"* I don't care who hears us as we consummate our strange friendship with each other. As a matter of fact, I hope everyone

in the building knows I'm fucking her. I hope they all know that I'm coming inside of her.

"Robert, oh fuck. Fuck." Mindy slows down as she looks down at me, her upper body dropping to mine as my cock is still buried inside of her twat. "Robert, that was fucking awesome." Her soft face on my chest causes goosebumps to rise up along my neck. I suddenly realize something as she lies here with me. I want her as more than just a lover or a friend. I want her with me forever. Lauren is less of a concern in my mind as I smell Mindy's fresh perfume.

"We've crossed a line," I say with a chuckle. "A very thick line that can't be uncrossed."

"I know," she replies quietly. "But I'm not giving you up." Mindy sits up to look into my eyes just as my cock finally slides out of her hole. "You're mine now, Robert, not hers. She can have Tim, but she will have to fight me for you. We need to make that clear to her."

As I look into her blue eyes, I can see that Mindy is serious about this statement of ownership. She feels that she has me now and that Lauren needs to relinquish title. I can agree with that right now, considering I feel the same way about her, but I still feel some attachment to my wife. Something, though, will have to change, and it's time we tell the other halves of our marriages about it.

Chapter Ten: No Easy Way

"You're fucking kidding," Lauren says as she shakes her head. "This is bullshit, Robert."

"Is it?" I hold up my cell phone as I scroll through the pictures that Tim has taken of her at other locations besides our house. "You're all about him now."

My wife looks over at Tim, but his eyes are affixed on his wife. "Tim, how did he get these pictures."

He looks back at Lauren and replies, "My brother, apparently."

"You've shared pics of me naked with someone else? Your *brother*? Why?" Lauren seems genuinely hurt by the idea that her lover might have given others access to a view of her body. Though she has become aware of the way I was sharing them last month with other men, this revelation that Tim has been sharing some pics of her seems to upset her even more.

"It was just a few, Lauren. They were harmless and I just wanted to share them, okay?" Tim looks over at Mindy and asks, "So he's the one you want now? After all we've been through?"

"Been through?" The young woman beside me shakes her head. "For more than two years I've sat back and watched you at work, Tim. I asked you to stop, but you wouldn't. You just had to have one more or had to work out your issues with someone other than me. I'm tired of you chasing hot wives all over the place. It's time we break it off."

Tim's eyes turn to me. "You've tried her out, haven't you?" I don't answer, but a kind of weird grin crosses his face. "I know, man, she's good. It's different to get some from another woman other than your wife, isn't it?"

"Look, Mindy is very sweet, Tim. She's full of life and you've been robbing her of that."

"I don't dispute that," he growls back. "But I don't want her anymore. I haven't wanted her for a while now and she knows that." His eyes focus on Mindy. "You know I don't like being married. It ties me down too much."

My wife looks at him and then at me. "Are you leaving me, Robert?"

"I don't know." I shake my head as I look at Mindy. "To be honest, Lauren, I still love you. But I don't want to be with you as much as I want to be with Mindy right now."

"So, would you want to stay married and have sex with her too? Would that make you happy?"

I look at Mindy, who replies, "I can live with us sharing him for now, Lauren, but I can't promise that I won't try to take him from you in the future. Robert is a special guy and I would love to have him to myself." The situation seems untenable and awkward at first. Mindy and I discussed the conflict I have of leaving my wife and taking up with another woman without at least some kind of time for closure. We both agreed that I could remain married for now if Lauren could agree to our terms, along with being sexually involved with each other. The fact is, I like sex with both women and I would really like to maintain that order for me for as long as I can.

"So, how would that work?" Lauren asks. "Robert stays married to me and you continue to have an affair with him?"

"Yes," Mindy answers flatly. "He loves you still, but I hope to convince him otherwise one day."

"Oh, really?" My wife gets up from her seat and looks down at me. She bends down in the floor in front of me and unfastens my pants.

"What are you doing?" I ask Lauren as she finally gets my dick out of my pants.

"I want to see just how bad you want her, Robert. I think you just wanted something from her because you've forgotten about me. I'm ready to show you what I can offer you if you dump her." Lauren stands up and pulls her skirt off, leaving her top on as she lowers her waxed muff down on my hard rod.

"Do you really want her to do that, Robert? Why are you hard?" Mindy runs her fingers through my hair. "Are you really going to let her fuck you?"

"Shit," I moan as my wife's wet snatch envelopes my cock. She begins to rock back and forth with me inside of her. "Damn, Lauren, what the fuck?"

"Yeah, what the fuck?" Tim looks at the two of us together. "So, what does this mean? Are you with me or not, Lauren?"

She turns and looks at him as her pussy juices begin to run all over my crotch. "He's a good fuck and I do love him, Tim. I want you too, but he's got to have something from me if I'm going to try to keep him."

Mindy begins to remove her clothes next to me, kissing me as my wife rides my cock. "Hang one, sweetie. I'll show you what's good." She smiles at me as she gets everything off and then settles next to me on the sofa. Mindy lowers her face to my chest and takes one of my nipples into her mouth, lapping at my areolas as she kisses and brushes against my chest. The feeling of two women paying such close attention to me causes me to get even harder.

Tim begins to take his tee shirt and shorts off, his cock already hard and ready for a hole. "Mindy, let me in." He walks up behind her and tugs at her ass.

"No!" she says as she turns from her husband. "I'm done with you."

"Let him," I plead with her as I watch the two of them together. "Let Tim come inside of you one last time, Mindy. I want to see what the two of you look like together when you fuck each other."

"Oh, Rob," my wife says as she bends down and kisses me.

Mindy looks at her husband for a moment before replying, "Once, Tim. Just this once." She goes back to nibbling on my chest, her ass in the air as her husband presses his cock against her hole. "Oh, damn," she moans as she feels him enter her from behind. Mindy looks into my eyes and says, "He's actually pretty good at this. I might come with him inside of me."

"I hope so." I reach up and gently caress her face as she kisses me deeply. My wife is now riding my cock while my lover is kissing me, her pussy being taken from behind by her own husband. This is beginning to be the sort of thing men's sex dreams are made up of.

"Oh, fuck," Lauren groans as she gets closer. "I'm going to burst." She begins to rock on top of me much harder, her wet labia slapping against my balls. "Rob...*Rob!*" My wife thunders suddenly into an orgasm as she runs her hands along my chest. *"Ohhh!!! AHHH!!!"* Lauren's petite body thrusts up and down on my rod hard as she squeals in unbelievable ecstasy. "Come inside of me, Robert. *Please COME IN ME!*" Her eyes look down into mine and I can see she's earnest about me coming inside of her, but I can't. I like being with her, and I like having her on me, but I don't want to come inside of my wife right now.

"I want in," I say to Tim as I look at him and Mindy. "I want in her ass."

"While I'm in her?"

"Yeah," I answer as my wife finishes her orgasm on me and rolls off. I look over at Lauren and smile as she nods at me. Tim stops to allow Mindy to turn around and sit down on me, her ass sliding slowly over my already lubricated man rod. She moves slowly at first as I spread her hips apart. But soon, Mindy is completely down on me and lying back against me as her husband fucks her pussy hard.

"Fucking hell, this is so *awesome,*" Mindy squeaks as both of our cocks work her holes out. I can feel him sliding in and out through the thin tissue separating her vagina from her anus, and the thought of having sex with her while another man is in her really turns me on.

"I'm going to lose it," I say as I get closer, her tight ass squeezing my penis hard. "You're really fucking tight in the ass, Mindy. So fucking tight."

"I'm..." Mindy begins to breathe hard as her fingers stroke her hard clitoris. "Oh, *FUCKKKK!!!*" Her small body suddenly turns pink as she goes into an explosive orgasm with two shafts working her holes.

"Ahhh...naaahhhhh!!!" I can feel each undulation as waves of orgasmic pleasure fill the young woman's body. She's fully into what we're doing with her as she comes.

"Uhhh!" Tim loses his load inside her wet hole as Mindy continues to climax, and he spurts hard enough that I can feel it through the thin walls of her anus and vagina. It causes me to begin to bust a nut into Mindy as well.

"Mindy...*mmmm!!!*" I spurt into her anus for the first time, each spurt feeling like she is too tight for me to pass my genetic soup into her ass. Mindy is much tighter than any other woman I've fucked in the ass, and I intensely enjoy putting my jism into her this way. *"Shit!!! FUCK!"* It takes a few more moments for me to finish just as Tim pulls out of her and I kiss Mindy on the neck and face. She rubs the side of my face with her fingers and after a moment of this we split apart, my cock wilting and slapping my balls as it comes out of her.

"That was good," Mindy says with a smile as both Tim's jism and mine rolls out from her holes down her legs.

"Very nice," Tim agrees as he goes over and kisses my wife.

As we all catch our breaths, I ask, "Is this the new normal for us?"

Lauren looks at the rest of us and answers, "I'm good with that for now. If that's okay with everyone else."

"Maybe," Mindy says as she looks at her husband. "But our marriage is over, Tim. I think we've known that for a while. I mean, I might fuck you once in a while, but I'm not living with you."

"Okay," Tim replies quietly. "I think I'm good with that. I just want to get a little sex whenever I can."

"And we well," I laughingly reply to him. "This could be good, but Lauren, I want to have Mindy move into our house. I want her to have a bedroom where I can visit her whenever I want to."

"Fine, but don't shut me out, okay? I'm still your wife." Lauren glares at me as I nod my head and take Mindy's hand. This is an odd arrangement, no doubt, but one I think that will help us all to become better people. Mindy gives me the sex I need away from Lauren and my wife gives me some sense of stability. I like both, so having each decide to work through it is exciting to me. It gives me more to hope for than when I sent a naked picture of Lauren to Tim. Who would have ever thought it would have ended up giving me another lover.

THE END

Sign up to my Patreon account and receive exclusive Hotwife stories every month and sexy scenes every week! https://www.patreon.com/karlyviolet

Don't miss out!

Visit the website below and you can sign up to receive emails whenever Karly Violet publishes a new book. There's no charge and no obligation.

https://books2read.com/r/B-A-GIXE-RFOJB

Did you love *Steamy Romance Opens Hotwife's Eyes - A Hot Wife Sordid Affair Wife Sharing Romance Novel*? Then you should read *Hotwife Sugar Book 1*[1] by Karly Violet and Scott Park!

Bored Housewife Seeking Older Rich Man For Intimacy!

Kevin stumbled across the Sugar Dating website and decided to browse to kill some timeThe website's motto was clear - Connecting Beautiful Women With Rich Men!As he scolled, Kevin had to admit the women were extraordinarily beautiful.And he was amazed by what he read, stunning women prepared to exchange time and intimacy for cash and security with an older and rich man.The number of attractive women was endless. And as he scrolled through the profiles, he couldn't believe just how many options a richer and older man had to choose room.One profile caught his eyes.........but it wasn't the tagline that

---

1. https://books2read.com/u/mV6XPp

2. https://books2read.com/u/mV6XPp

stopped him in his tracks........Bored housewife seeking rich man for no strings attached intimacy!It was the fact that the woman looked very much like his wife.*And in fact, on closer inspection - the curious husband was certain the profile belonged to his wife.***What would you do if you found your wife on a Sugar Dating website?***This scorching hot novel is part 1 of the series 'Hotwife Sugar' and features adultery, a cheating wife and a husband refusing to believe the rumours and the hard evidence of his wife playing away from home*

About the Author

Sign up to my mailing list to receive the two free epilogues for 'A Hotwife Adventure' and 'Hotwife Training' and to stay up to date on all of my latest releases! http://eepurl.com/c3ICWf Sign up to my Patreon account and receive exclusive Hotwife stories every month and sexy scenes every week! https://www.patreon.com/karlyviolet

Read more at https://www.patreon.com/karlyviolet.

About the Publisher

www.ingramcontent.com/pod-product-compliance
Lightning Source LLC
Chambersburg PA
CBHW020119180726
47992CB00019B/1032